NEXT VOICE YOU HEAR

C.G. SPENCER

ISBN: 978-1-954614-17-8 hard cover
ISBN: 978-1-954614-18-5 soft cover

Edited by: Monika Dziamka

Published by Warren Publishing
Charlotte, NC
www.warrenpublishing.net
Printed in the United States

AUTHOR'S NOTE:

The events associated with the Tritium facilities are in no way real. They are pure fiction and cannot and will not ever happen. Those facilities are, in my opinion, the best-run nuclear facilities in the world and I am proud to have had the privilege to work there.

Classification review was completed and approval given for uncontrolled release.

*This book is dedicated to my mother. I've spent a good deal of
time in memory care facilities, interacting with the wonderful
residents and caregivers. During that time, I watched my loving,
Christian mother change as she progressed through the phases
of her dementia. She spent her life giving to others, doing things
like herding runny-nosed children into church buses on Sunday
morning, praying for me as God rescued me from myself,
and on and on. Virtually all the situations in the book are ones
I witnessed firsthand, though they are not all necessarily
associated with my mother. I wrote this book to try and
answer my own question: "where has Mom gone?"*

I love you, Mom. See you soon.

Thank You
*Thank you to my family for allowing me to write this book and
thanks to Richard, Deb, and Rich for encouraging me along the way.*

Seeing things somewhat more clearly now, though not entirely yet, I'm going to tell you about some of the events that occurred while I was entangled in a body on Earth. Critical though this test-period existence was to my eternal fate, most of the things that seemed important there were really insignificant when compared to where I am now. Though that may sound callous and insensitive, it remains true.

On Earth I made many mistakes, but not understanding who and where I was and often fearing the wrong things—those were my biggest. Hopefully this story will help you discover who you are and gain perspective. Occasionally, like now, I will address you directly to help clarify the events that occur. I'll begin the story in what may seem a sad place, though it really wasn't, for it led me to a place now that is perfect and I want you to join me.

OLD HABITS
Fall Leaves (2012)

I t was morning, and he was just waking up. Last night had been rough. He'd gotten out of bed to urinate and fallen. After crawling to the bathroom, pulling himself up by the sink, and doing his business, he used the wall to get back into bed. The room smelled like urine. In truth, it smelled like urine everywhere in the facility. Craig wasn't the only resident who struggled with incontinence.

He opened his eyes and looked around the room. *Where am I?* he thought. *Hell, who am I?*

I would have liked to help, but I couldn't. You see, the dementia had by then already severely damaged my connection. I knew exactly what he thought and felt but couldn't control any of it anymore. He was shorting out. Sure, at times I could get through and run things again, but it was maybe once a day, at most. Sometimes when our daughter Katy came by, there was still enough of a connection generated that I could access his mind and put out a few words of love to her. But it only lasted a few minutes. Then what I call the preprogrammed software took over. It was actually a great software program with a good physical network that had learned much from his life—learned from his childhood, his education, his faith, his college experiences, his time with his family, and so on.

He had been very successful in his job, marriage, fatherhood, and life in general. However, he loved to drink too much, which often led him astray. He was also often proud, self-serving, and manipulative. I had my hands full keeping him in line. Hell, I had a hard time keeping myself in line. I too loved the things he loved and enjoyed both the good and the bad. We had some great times in college and in those few years after graduation, but I shouldn't dwell on those because they weren't right. The good times were when we lived right, when I could suppress our bad desires.

The door opened and broke the silence. It was Shana, Craig's caregiver. She was all business.

"Time to get up, Mr. Craig. You need a shower this morning, so I'll get Thomas to come in and help you."

"I already had my shower," he replied. "Don't need another damn shower! Get out of here and let me sleep."

"No, Mr. Craig, you need to get up and get a shower. It's Thursday, and breakfast will be ready in half an hour." Shana left and closed the door behind her.

Craig sighed, kicked the covers off, and sat up in bed. He had no idea where he was. His mind was chaotic. Thoughts came and went quickly, bouncing around wildly like a lottery ball drawing. He knew they were there but had trouble grasping them. When he did grab hold of a thought, it was only for a moment, and then he lost it. He usually couldn't make anything of it and couldn't connect it to anything else. Wondering where he was, he stood up and balanced unsteadily on skinny legs, his T-shirt and boxers wrinkled and saggy like the skin over his knees. His legs were used so seldom these days. Not like before. He used to be in great shape—a man who loved to run. A man who could squat 450 pounds. A man who used to have great wheels, not these scrawny chicken legs.

He made his way toward the bathroom, shuffling across the low-pile carpet toward the cold tile and noticing the new dent in the drywall. His fall last night caused it, but he, of course, had no recollection of it. His eyes next went to the mirror, and what he saw shocked him. He ran his hand through his gray hair, staring at the face he no longer recognized as his own.

The door opened again as Thomas walked into his room. Thomas was a nice young man. He stood six feet tall and weighed a lean and well-defined two hundred pounds, and his hair was cropped short with sharp lines forming points above his temples. He wore a snug-fitting Fall Leaves golf shirt that readily showed his build, pressed khakis, and suede, tan-colored work boots. His body was in sharp contrast to his personality, which was gentle and tender. Raised by a disciplined but loving father, Thomas had learned to fear God, work hard, and don humility. Though he hadn't gone to college after high school, Thomas loved to read and was attending evening classes at the local University of Georgia branch.

"Mr. Craig, it's Thomas. Come to help you get a shower."

"I don't need no shower, boy. I already had one."

"No, you didn't, Mr. Craig. The last one you had was Sunday when your daughter Katy was here. She helped you, remember?"

"Ah, bull—," he muttered. "I already had my shower this morning and you can't make me take another. Now get outta here before I thump you!"

"That's no way to be, Mr. Craig. I would never make you do anything. I just want to help you. You need a shower because you're going home today. You want to look your best when Katy comes to get you."

There it was—Thomas's main ploy. He told the residents anything he wanted, knowing that within minutes they'd forget every word he'd said.

"Come on, Mr. Craig. Let me help you."

"Am I really going home today?"

"Yes, Mr. Craig, you are. Back to Aiken, where you live."

"Oh, that's great. I hate it here. Okay then. Come on in. I'll get a shower."

Thomas helped Craig out of his clothes while the water got warm. Craig hated the feel of water on his skin, especially his head. Regardless of the temperature, the shower always felt cold to Craig, the drops of water like little needles that sent tiny shivers as they hit. Thomas took Craig by the arm and led him to the three-inch lip that kept the water from going all over the floor. Craig raised his foot to step in and then put it right back down.

"I don't need no f— shower!" he roared, his eyes now filled with rage. "Why are you making me take another shower, you Black bastard?"

"It's okay, Mr. Craig," Thomas replied. "You have to get ready to go home today. Katy is coming after breakfast to get you."

"She is? Why didn't someone tell me? Am I going back to Aiken or to Cleveland?"

"Aiken," Thomas replied. "Your new house is ready and Katy is picking you up. Now, let's get washed up."

Craig stepped into the shower.

By 7:30 in the morning, many of the residents were already seated in the dining room, though breakfast wouldn't be served for at least half an hour. The facility itself was nice, having been built two years prior. The furniture was new and the walls tastefully decorated with paintings of winter landscapes, peaceful cottages, and carefree families.

Fall Leaves had three floors. The first floor was an assisted living facility where residents were free to come and go. The memory care wings occupied the second and third floors. Craig was on the second floor, Emerald Hall, a dementia unit for those with severe cognitive decline. All doors were locked, but oddly enough residents rarely tried to get out. Most remained on the second floor, oblivious to life outside the halls. The third floor, the Pearl, was reserved for residents whose dementia was even more progressed. It was a despairing place.

The internal wiring of Pearl residents was totally shorted out, and their software packages, no matter how sophisticated, couldn't get their ganglia to fire on command. Pearl residents had no access to memory files and were run by their subconscious packages—you know, the software that makes you scratch an itch or take a leak.

Meals for all three floors were prepared on floor one in the Fall Leaves kitchen. Around eight each morning, employees stacked the prepared breakfast trays onto carts and loaded the meals into the elevator to send to the Emerald floor. The residents generally waited in their seats in the floor's modest dining room, blankly staring into space or at the TV screens on the wall. Their lottery balls of thought bounced around their brains, hoping to be caught by their consciousness for a moment of focus. Most seemed at peace.

Shana stood behind the counter waiting quietly. She was in her early thirties and had another job. This one paid $16.75 an hour, and though she was dedicated to helping the residents at Fall Leaves and felt a strong sense of service for the elderly, she was not going to get hurt or take any unnecessary risks. She knew the rules and stuck to them, a compliance-based employee. That is, she knew what she could and couldn't do and stayed well inside those boundaries. For example, she would never have done what Thomas did this morning. Shana would never have lied to get someone into the shower. If a patient refuses a request, leave the room. Don't cause a scene. That was her approach. The only way to get in trouble was to be charged with coercing or restraining the residents. Family members could deal with resistant and stubborn residents, not Shana. She looked out into the dining room, making sure everyone who needed to be there was indeed accounted for.

The large-screen TV on the wall was tuned to CNN. About half of the seated residents looked at the screen with blank stares. Betty Lewis was one of them. The news commentator was discussing Facebook going public.

"Facebook is going public," Betty muttered and looked at the table. The news played on. She glanced up. A few minutes passed before she repeated, "They're going public." Again, she looked down at the table.

Betty was wearing a designer jogging suit with designer tennis shoes. She'd made an attempt to comb her hair but she'd missed the flat spot in the back, evidence of how she'd slept. The dye job was a pretty shade of brunette, but didn't cover the gray roots.

Betty had been a beautiful woman. She was sixty-two, slender, and physically fit. She had only worked for three years after majoring in chemical engineering. Her marriage to Tom and the birth of their first son, Levi, ended her career as she chose to become a full-time mom. Over the next two decades, she and Tom raised three boys. She was a caring mother and wife. Tom was a lawyer for a large firm in Atlanta, where he was still a practicing partner. He'd made partner in just four years, brilliant and well-respected in the firm. However, Tom was a bit of a scoundrel. While he loved Betty, he'd had several affairs over the years. Betty had some knowledge of them but always forgave Tom. However, four years ago, just at the onset of her dementia, Tom became involved with another attorney at his firm and filed for divorce. Betty was, of course, devastated, but the dementia dulled the pain.

Two of Betty's sons lived out of state. Her second son, Michael, was in California, and her youngest, David, lived in Montana. Levi was still in Atlanta and was Betty's main caregiver. All three boys loved Betty, but Levi did all the work. He visited regularly, bought her clothes, and watched out for her. The other two boys seldom visited. They were torn by the divorce but stayed in close contact with their father. Levi, however, had broken all contact with his father. He despised the man who'd cheated on his mom for years and then left her for another woman when his mother needed him most. How could his brothers even stand to talk to him? Levi's resolve was to care for his mother no matter what.

Seated next to Betty was Olga. Olga was of German descent, loved to speak of her homeland, and was a bit brash and loud. She had broad shoulders and long gray hair that still had traces of blonde. She stared at the open *Wall Street Journal* her husband had delivered daily to the facility but looked up when Betty made her second statement about Facebook. Annoyed by the interruption, she said, "So what?" then looked back down at her paper. Olga read the words, but they were meaningless to her. Even though she could understand them, Olga couldn't put them in the context of the story. She read the words of her paper for over an hour each day without comprehension. However, somehow she sensed that having this practice was part of who she was, so her ritual continued.

Betty looked up as Shana stood next to her with two plates in her hand. The food had arrived from downstairs. Each plate contained a biscuit, scrambled eggs, and a piece of bacon. As Betty smiled, Shana said, "Breakfast is here, Miss Betty," and put the plate in front of her. "Do you want some coffee?"

"Yes, please."

"Do you want orange or cranberry juice, Miss Betty?" Ten seconds awkwardly passed as Betty contemplated the big decision. "Orange or cranberry, Miss Betty?" The pause continued. Shana took a glass of orange juice from the cart behind her and set it in front of Betty.

"Thank you," Betty responded.

Shana then placed the second plate in front of Olga. Olga looked up and said, "I'm reading the paper."

Shana said, "I know, Miss Olga. You read it every day, don't you?"

"Of course I do. I need to know what's going on. I stay informed so that I can run my business."

"Of course," Shana replied. "Do you want cranberry or orange juice this morning?"

Olga said, "Yes, coffee please."

Shana put a glass of cranberry juice in front of Olga and turned away. She had been instructed to ask and she had. She was always compliant.

Back in his room, Craig was getting out of the shower and Thomas was helping him dry off. He had laid out pants, a shirt, and boxers on the bed.

"Let's go get dressed for breakfast," Thomas said. Craig slowly shuffled to his bed and sat down. He was naked and shivering from the shower.

"Why am I naked?" he asked.

"You just had a nice shower, Mr. Craig," Thomas responded. "Let's get dressed for breakfast." He handed Craig his boxers, and Craig put them on.

After Craig had dressed himself with Thomas's assistance, he shuffled back into the bathroom and looked into the mirror. His gray hair was matted to his head. He took the comb on the counter and combed it forward.

"Let me help you," Thomas said and took the comb from Craig's hand. He parted it on the side and combed it as he did each day. "You've still got it, Mr. Craig," Thomas said with a sincere smile.

"Got what?" Craig responded. "Why the hell are you combing my hair? I've got to get out of here! I have to be at work."

"Of course, Mr. Craig, but let's get some breakfast first."

Thomas went to the other room and returned with the black walker that sat at the end of the bed and put it in front of Craig.

"I don't need a damn walker! I can walk on my own."

"Of course you can," Thomas replied. "The doctor just wants you to use it until your hip completely heals."

"What's wrong with my hip?"

"You broke it skiing, Mr. Craig."

"I did?" Craig asked.

"Yes, Mr. Craig. You're a great skier, but even the best get hurt occasionally."

"Oh," Craig said and took hold of the walker.

Thomas knew he had lied and broken the company policy stating that employees were not to intentionally mislead the residents. Thomas ignored the policy at his own peril. He truly cared about Craig and hated when he got upset. He ignored the coarse, sometimes racist, and frequently hurtful comments Craig made. It was the disease talking. Not Craig.

I loved Thomas. Though he didn't really fully understand what was going on, his Spirit led him to do what was right. That took not only courage, but self-denial and forbearance. He had my respect.

When Thomas and Craig arrived at the dining hall, the other residents were being served. Thomas put Craig at the table with Betty and Olga. "You know Miss Olga and Miss Betty, Mr. Craig. You get to sit with two pretty young ladies this morning."

Craig let go of the walker, slowly turned, then sat down. Thomas held the solid wood chair and helped scoot Craig up to the table. "I'll leave you with Miss Olga and Miss Betty now," he said as he turned and walked away.

Craig stared off into space, confused at what was happening. His mind tried to lock into where he was and what he was doing, but it was useless.

I could only watch.

Betty was shyly looking down at her plate, avoiding eye contact and stabbing at her food. Her hands were unsteady, but she could still cut her food and eat by herself. Olga looked up from her paper and said, "Who are you?" Craig looked at her with a blank expression. His eyes surveyed her. She was not that attractive. Craig felt nothing and said nothing. After a few seconds Olga said, "Hmmph" and resumed reading the paper.

Shana approached Craig with his breakfast. "Orange or cranberry juice, Mr. Craig?" she asked. Craig said nothing. Shana didn't ask twice; she just sat a glass of orange juice in front of him and walked back to the counter where the remaining trays of food were.

Craig began to eat his food. As he was doing so, he fixed his gaze on Betty. Looking her over, Craig had an immediate mental reaction. He wasn't exactly sure what he felt, but he liked it.

"Hello," he said to Betty as he smiled across the table.

Betty looked up at Craig and stared for a few seconds. She smiled shyly and looked back down at her plate.

"Hello," he said again. "Who are you?"

Betty was embarrassed but looked up at Craig again.

"Betty," she said and again looked down.

"Betty, huh? Well, Betty, you sure are a nice-looking woman." Craig's brain had started firing. His mind was lit up with activity, and he was feeling good. He knew something was going on but wasn't sure what it meant. Betty turned red and looked into Craig's blue eyes.

"Thank you," she said almost in a whisper. "Your name is Craig, right?" Somehow, she'd remembered his name. She wasn't sure where it came from, but she said it anyway.

"That's right," Craig said. "I'm Craig."

He took another bite of food and added, "I'm going home soon," though he was uncertain of why he said it. "My daughter Katy is building me a house in Aiken. It's a beautiful house, and it will have all my furniture in it. I need to get home so I can get to work. I don't know why I'm here, but I know I'm going home."

"That's great," Betty said, reaching for her glass of juice. "I think I may go home soon too. Why *are* we here?" she asked Craig.

At this, Olga slammed down her paper and glared at them both. "I come here for breakfast each day and you two do the same," she said. "We always eat breakfast here, and I always read my paper so I can know how to manage my business. I need to get out of here after I eat this. I only live a few blocks away. This food is good, but I may not be back." Olga snatched her paper from the table and shook it, making a sharp clapping sound.

Craig ignored Olga's diatribe and kept his gaze on Betty. He couldn't take his eyes off her and wanted desperately to be with her. He wasn't sure why, but he did. The attraction was strong. "You are a nice-looking woman," Craig repeated, having no idea he had already said it.

"Thank you," Betty whispered again and looked down at her plate once more to ease her embarrassment.

I knew what was happening. Craig had always had a strong libido, and he'd developed skills to assure it was satisfied. If I'm honest, I'd enjoyed the fruits of Craig's labor. So my initial thought was, Go get her, Craig. Then, no; Betty's vulnerable and Craig's in no mental shape to have an affair. (Still, I thought, I wouldn't mind seeing Betty undressed and in the sack.)

Craig just kept staring at Betty and continued to eat his breakfast. Soon a look of surprise came over his face as another beautiful woman appeared before him. Craig looked up at her. She seemed to Craig to be in her early thirties, with long brown hair and large blue eyes. She wore a fairly conservative suit, which included a fitted blue skirt, a pressed white shirt, and a blue coat. Her legs were muscled and slightly tanned.

"Hey, Dad," she said.

Craig's brain began to fire again, and memory connected.

"Hi, Katy. How are you doing, you beautiful, smart daddy's girl? You're my favorite daughter." It was an automatic response for Craig. Certain things, like Katy's coming, set off a firestorm in his brain, and he could access memory to immediately know who she was, how to respond, and even be able to joke a bit.

Katy, Craig's only child, was thirty-nine but looked younger. She was a partner at Samuels, Stone, and McBrier, a large law firm in Atlanta, and married to Mark. They had a twelve-year-old daughter, Cameron. Katy was incredibly smart and always impeccably dressed. She had a quick wit, flavored with generally tasteful sarcasm. However, when confronted, that wit and sarcasm could be deadly. She had grown up in Chagrin Falls, Ohio, finished fourth in her high school class of over five hundred students, and carried a 3.9 GPA all of her life, including during her undergraduate work at Ohio State, where she also attended law school.

Katy's undergraduate work was in pre-med, but she'd decided her senior year that medicine was not really for her. She had called Craig just after midterm exams and sprung the news that she no longer wanted to be a doctor. Medicine was too straightforward, and she needed a career to better use her logic and debating skills. These were the skills that Craig had helped her hone over the years through family debates on everything from politics to allowing alcohol at high school parties.

Craig had known immediately what to do. He simply complimented her on her logic skills and then went into the merits and pitfalls of her new career choice. And after a long discussion, Katy decided to make the change and go to law school, and go she did. She aced the LSAT, and with her 3.9 GPA in pre-med, she was accepted into the OSU Moritz College of Law in the first round. Samuels, Stone, and McBrier had given her an immediate offer after she passed the bar.

"What's for breakfast, Dad?" she asked, looking down at Craig's plate. Craig no longer did well with questions. Staring at his plate, he paused.

"Well, I guess it's eggs and other stuff."

"Good, Dad," Katy responded. "Did you sleep well last night?" Katy knew that she shouldn't ask Craig questions about the recent past but she always groped for things to say once the initial greeting had occurred. Doing so often sent Craig into another place.

"I guess so," he said. "I don't know why I am staying here. I want to go home, back to Aiken. I miss my home. Are you going to take me back to Aiken?"

Katy immediately felt her stress level rise. She knew the question had sent Craig back to one of his remaining sources for strong memories, to Aiken, South Carolina.

"Why have you put me here?" Craig asked. "Did you sell my house in Aiken?"

Craig had been in Fall Leaves for nearly three years. Katy had made the arrangements herself and sold the family house in Aiken. Her mother, Anne, had died from cancer two years before Katy moved him, and the decision still haunted her.

Katy knew this predicament all too well. When Craig's hardware first began to short out, Katy had refused to realize and accept what was happening. *God wouldn't do that to my dad. He just wouldn't,* she'd thought. *There's no way my dad is getting dementia. He's too smart and has been a good Christian since childhood. God can't be that cruel. No way.*

She kept that frame of mind despite her mother's continual warnings about her father not being all right. Anne told Katy how forgetful he was becoming.

"Old age does that," Katy responded.

"Yes, but your dad is cursing again, talking like he did in college," Anne told her. "He is so coarse and never does his devotions anymore, at least not daily as he did his entire adult life."

Despite the signs, Katy refused to accept Craig's fate even after a day in her life that should have made it impossible to ignore. One day, early in Craig's progression, Katy was in Augusta for a deposition. She'd just begun her legal career and had a grueling day. So, she did what she loved most to do to destress—she called her father.

At first, he was just her dad. "Hey, Katy, whatcha doin'? Beating some poor slob into verbal submission?" This was the dad she knew, always complimentary.

Katy always understood how much we loved her and how very proud we were of her. We bragged continuously about our girl. We'd even tell strangers about her GPA, about her first-round acceptance to law school, about skipping med school to practice law. She was daddy's girl, all right, and we were proud.

Katy said, "Yeah, Dad, I beat 'em up pretty bad today. Hey, I'd love to see you. I've got a hotel room here in Augusta, but would it be okay if I spent the night with you and Mom? I could get up early, come back to Augusta, and finish my last depositions before I head back to Atlanta tomorrow."

"Uh, sure," Craig said. "What time will you be here? I'll put some pasta on and have it ready for you when you get here. Mom made her famous sauce and meatballs yesterday, and I can make you a nice salad too."

"That would be great. Is Mom there?"

"No. I think she just left for her weekly ladies' Bible study. You and I can eat and get caught up before the old girl gets back."

"Dad," Katy had said, "that's not nice."

"You're right. She's just a little old. I'll see you in about forty-five minutes?"

"Make it an hour. I need to check out first."

"Okay, baby. I'll see you soon."

Katy walked from the law office to the hotel across the street. She went upstairs, packed her things in her overnight bag, and checked out of the hotel. During her drive, she replayed and mulled over the conversation. Dad had been a bit hesitant about her visit. Did he have something else planned? Was he worried about something? She sensed that Craig was not his usual self. *Not to worry*, she thought. *I'll help him deal with whatever is bothering him when I get there.*

When she arrived, Katy lightly knocked on the door and then, realizing it was unlocked, opened it to the formal entryway. The floor was white marble with an antique table holding an ornate stained-glass lamp. Katy set her bag beside the table directly below a picture of her in her wedding gown. The house had the smell of freshly cut flowers. That smell and the familiar click of her bag hitting the marble floor somehow caused a peaceful feeling to come over her. She was home and safe.

"I'm here, Dad," she called out, to no response. She walked down the hall and then over to Craig, who was standing in the middle of the kitchen, holding their dog, Luke. Craig nuzzled his face into Luke's fluffy, white poodle fur as the dog wagged his tail at Katy.

"How ya doing?" Craig asked, still clinging to Luke and making no attempt to hug Katy. He just looked over with a gaze that stunned her. He then turned and went into the living room and sat on the couch. Katy's shock grew. There was no hug; there was no pasta dinner. There was just Dad, looking confused and awkward.

Is it true? she thought. *Is Dad sick, or is this just a senior moment?* Tears instantly filled her eyes. *Was Mom right?*

At Fall Leaves, Katy shook off the memory and knew immediately how to respond to Craig's question about moving him into the facility. She had learned from experience and from discussions with Craig's doctor that confrontation should be avoided whenever possible.

"Sure, Dad," she said, now with practiced confidence. "We sold the house after Mom passed because it was too big, then you moved into your apartment here. I'm building you a new house, remember?"

"Is it in Aiken or back in Cleveland?" Craig asked.

"It's in Aiken, just like you wanted."

"Good," Craig responded. "Is it almost done?"

"Yes," Katy replied, placing her hand gently on his shoulder. "All the furniture you and Mom had is going in soon, and the house should be ready soon."

"Aww, Katy. You're so good to me," Craig said and took another bite of toast. "You're my best girl, and I love you."

Katy's response somehow caused Craig's brain to fire well enough to remember his love for her. *I had nothing to do with it; it was all software talking. But I was grateful for it anyway. It made our girl Katy smile. That was enough for me.*

Katy hated lying, especially to Craig. She'd tried being truthful before, and it resulted in a complete meltdown, with Craig showing a side she had never seen. When he first moved to Fall Leaves, Craig interrogated Katy relentlessly. "Where is my car? Did you sell my house? Where am I? Why am I here?" Katy calmly reminded him that Anne had passed away and that he could no longer drive. She patiently told him that he wasn't able to care for himself any longer and that was why he was in his new apartment, surrounded by nice people who could help him. Craig had gone nonlinear, piercing Katy with a hardened countenance she had never seen before. His gaze was evil. Craig's blue eyes squinted tightly and seemed to look right through her.

"You ass," he spat at her. "You sold my house and kept the money. I can drive and I'll show you. How could you have done this to me? You've taken everything from me and locked me away in this God-forsaken place!"

Katy had been terrified and teared up, but she let him rave. *Who is this?* she thought. *Where is my dad?* His harsh words and steely eyes never left her, and from that day on she was determined to do whatever it took to keep that surreal event from happening again.

The truth was that Anne had been his caregiver during the early phases of his sickness. Although he had not been diagnosed with dementia, his wife knew he was failing, so she cared and covered for him. *I hated that time. Anne was such a wonderful wife and mother, and we loved her more than anything else in the world.* However, during Craig's early progression, except for her conversations with Katy, Anne did everything she could to hide it and protect Craig. It was a burden she bore alone.

Later in Craig's progression, as if the burden of Craig's illness wasn't enough, Anne was diagnosed with breast cancer. It was caught late, and she passed within a couple of years. Prior to Anne's death, Katy put all the assets in a trust she'd created, with herself as the trustee. Anne had wanted Katy to do so, or at least she agreed to it, believing Katy knew best due to her legal experience. Craig had always managed the legal and financial affairs of the family before he became ill, but Anne had been more than willing for Katy to take over.

As the dementia got worse, Katy had been torn like never before. Should she move us into a dementia unit? But how could she? Those places smelled, and people drooled. They were cuckoo nests. She wanted to take care of us but realized it was impossible. She'd have to quit her job and neglect her husband and daughter. Her logical side told her it was simply not feasible, but the guilt and the pain of it is still with her today.

So, Katy lied. It was the only way to keep her dad from assuming that evil look again and flying into fits of rage. Morally, her deception didn't sit well with her, but she knew it had to be done.

She lied, and she lied often. *I hated to see Katy so conflicted, but I was proud of her for doing what was right. God could not have wanted her to ignite Craig's software. No way. I only wished that I could somehow have communicated to her that I understood and agreed.*

"I see you're eating with Olga and Betty this morning, Dad."

Craig paused and looked around, no longer aware of who sat near him.

"Hmm" was his only response.

Katy knew both Olga and Betty, or at least she knew about them. She looked at Olga and asked, "What's new in the news today?"

Olga peered over her newspaper and looked at Katy as though she had just interrupted a teacher grading papers.

"Facebook is going public," she replied. The sentence had stuck in her brain after Betty's comment just a few minutes earlier. Olga actually had no idea what she was reading in the paper.

"Oh, yes," said Katy. "I guess they are." Katy followed politics and current events because she felt she had to. She needed to be able to respond in partner meetings and stay up-to-date in proceedings, but she did not like it. It seemed to her that most politicians were useless. Their only drive was for party, power, and reelection.

Olga gave Katy another somewhat-annoyed gaze and continued reading.

"And how are you, Betty?" she asked, turning her body slightly to better face the sweet woman.

Betty looked up with a humble smile and stared at Katy.

"You're very beautiful. Do I know you?"

"Yes," Katy replied, smiling back. "We've met. You and my dad are friends."

"We are?" she asked.

Katy saw the fruitlessness of the discussion and sat down at the table, watching as Betty and Craig slowly finished their breakfasts.

Olga was eating too, but only an occasional bite. She'd look away from her paper and nod knowingly, as if she had just gained great insight. Her software was performing the same functions it had done most of her life. The difference was that now it was simply automatic and had no real relevance.

Katy looked around the room. At the table next to theirs was a woman who looked to be in her late seventies. She was eating her food and watching the television. She said nothing and made no response as Katy said hello to her. The man seated next to the woman was bent forward, leaning over his plate, drool dripping from his mouth and swinging back and forth from his chin. Katy quickly looked away and tried to settle the queasy feeling in the pit of her stomach.

Looks like the caregivers should feed this poor fellow, she thought. In fact, she was right; he was supposed to have assistance with eating. What that meant to the compliance-based caregivers, however, was that they were to give him a fork, chop his food, and occasionally ask if he needed help. His usual response was to stare ahead.

How does this poor guy exist if he doesn't eat? Katy thought. *Why don't these lazy people come and help him?* Katy thought about doing it herself, but she knew it would start a fight with the staff and wouldn't be a long-term solution to the problem. She hoped he had a family who would be checking in on him.

After being at the table for about five more minutes, Katy rose, saying she had to leave, but she'd be back soon.

Craig regarded her with a questioning look. "Okay," he said. He had forgotten she was even there.

Katy gave him a hug and then walked down the corridor into Craig's room. It smelled like urine and stale skin. The bed had been made, but crumbs littered the carpet. Craig loved sweets, so on her weekend visits, Katy often brought and left cookies. His favorite was chocolate chip, but the chocolate stained his sheets and carpet so the crumbs were oatmeal, his second favorite. She walked into the bathroom and pulled back the shower curtain. It was wet. That was good. Perhaps her father had actually showered this morning. As she looked around the bathroom, she heard a knock at the door.

"Anyone in here?" Thomas called out.

"It's just me, Thomas."

"Hey, Katy," Thomas responded. He had actually watched Katy come into the room and wanted to talk to her.

"I got your dad to take a shower this morning. I know how you like to be aware of those things. It went pretty well. I had to tell him he was going home to make it happen, but it worked."

Katy smiled at Thomas. "You're a saint, Thomas. I don't know how you do it, but I can't thank you enough for caring about my dad. It means more to me than you will ever know."

Thomas smiled back at Katy. "I love Mr. Craig. I know he's a good man and loves God like I do. His mind is just out of whack, but when he's at peace, he's a pleasure. I can tell he was very smart, and he did such a great job raising you."

"Has he said anything hurtful to you recently?"

Thomas hesitated for a minute, struggling with revealing the truth to her.

"Oh, those occasional inappropriate things aren't really your dad. They don't bother me in the least. I know he likes me. It's just that he occasionally becomes a different person. I ignore that person, and with a little love I'm usually able to bring the real Mr. Craig back."

"You're a saint, Thomas. A true saint," Katy repeated. She was truly horrified at what her dad said from time to time. She had heard him drop the "F" bomb and use the "N" word when asking about Thomas and other Black caregivers. It not only embarrassed her, but it scared her too. How could she expect these caregivers to ever care for her dad? She wouldn't blame them if they ignored him, or worse. She had no idea where his behavior came from. Her dad had never been racist, at least not to her knowledge. He'd always supported minority causes and taught her about what was right.

I knew where it came from. It was part of Craig's package from the start, though it had deepened as his software picked up comments from others. It came from friends and acquaintances, who voiced their opinions. Those comments formed logic paths in his brain. I had always been able to control those thoughts and keep them at bay. I knew they were wrong. However, the program now controlled him, and there was little I could do, except wait for one of the occasional, small moments of clarity to try and correct what he had done.

For instance, one Sunday, Craig attended the morning worship session in the conference room. The assistant pastor from a local church, a lady named Heidi, was singing "Amazing Grace" when Craig's brain suddenly began to fire correctly again. He teared up and was immediately at peace. Thomas was seated next to Craig and was singing as well. I seized the moment and took over. He looked over at Thomas, and I made him say, "I love you, Thomas. You're a good man." Thomas stopped singing and acted like he'd just seen an angel. He was speechless for a moment and then said, "Mr. Craig, I love you too," and then he began to cry. Now that's a success story.

Katy glanced once more around the room and said, "Well, I better get going. I've got to be in court in an hour."

"You the woman!" Thomas said in response. "Your dad is so proud of you. I hope you understand that and know that he loves you so very much. When he's in one of his peaceful moods, I sometimes take that picture of you from the shelf and ask him who it is. He almost always knows it's you. Sometimes he will just open up and start bragging about you. He tells me about law school and how smart you are."

A tear ran down Katy's face. "Thank you, Thomas," she said. Katy gave him a long hug and then Thomas walked her to the elevator.

***

Back in the dining room, Craig was finishing his breakfast, as were Olga and Betty. Craig was sitting in his chair and staring again at Betty. Suddenly, he had a burst of memory. It was sex. He could remember what it was like, and he was enjoying it. His drive was back again. He looked at Betty, not really knowing exactly who she was, but he knew he needed to be with her. *Uh-oh. We're headed for trouble. I tried so hard to slam on the brakes, but it was useless.*

"Is your name Betty?" he asked.

Betty shyly looked up at Craig. "Yes. It is."

"Well, you sure are a beautiful woman." Craig turned on the charm.

"Thank you." A tentative smile began to spread across her face.

"Why don't you come to my room with me? We can watch some TV or just talk," Craig said.

Betty was immediately taken back to her past. Though she couldn't really remember the occasion, her brain let her know she had been here before and that it was exciting.

"Okay," she agreed.

Craig pushed his chair back from the table and tried to stand. It took him several attempts, but he finally made it. Betty stood as well, while Olga remained seated, still reading her paper.

"This way," Craig said, slowly walking toward his room.

The caregivers watched from the counter area but did nothing, focusing instead on their next task—cleaning the breakfast dishes. Craig and Betty continued down the hall. Without his walker, Craig's pace was slow and unsteady. Betty followed behind with her head bent.

Craig opened the door and held it for Betty as she entered somewhat hesitantly. The room was manly and functional. A leather love seat faced the window. A recliner and double bed faced a small LED TV on the wall. Katy had chosen and arranged the furniture.

"Sit down," Craig said to Betty. "Sit here on this couch."

Betty meekly sat down on the love seat, her heart beating fast though she was unsure why. Craig was confused too. Where should he sit? Should he go ahead and sit next to Betty or sit in his recliner? His brain was telling him to sit next to Betty. *Yes! Craig chose the recliner, much to my relief. Maybe I could get some run time and keep this thing from going south.*

Craig stared at Betty. Suddenly he remembered why he had invited this girl to his room. His software began to fire again. "You are very beautiful," he said.

"Thank you," Betty responded, as if it was the first time Craig had said it.

"Very beautiful," Craig said again. Betty focused her attention on the carpet. She had nothing on her mind, nothing at all.

Craig was now firing on all cylinders, canned cylinders. He began to rock in the recliner. He rocked again, pushed down on the arms with his triceps, and stood to his feet. He slowly walked over to the love seat and sat next to Betty. Neither said a word. Both were operating on autopilot. After about a minute of silence and blank stares at the wall, Craig turned his head to look at Betty. She didn't meet his gaze. Craig reached for her hand, and she finally looked up at him. *It's on, and I can't stop it.*

Craig lightly squeezed Betty's hand while she gazed into his eyes. He began to rock again, and while holding Betty's right hand in his left, he pushed off the arm of the couch and stood to his feet. Betty followed. Craig's instincts took over. He had been here before, though he couldn't remember any specifics. He led Betty to the bed, placed his hands on her shoulders, and moved in to give her a kiss. She was gazing straight ahead and let it happen. He softly pressed down on her shoulders so that she would sit on the bed. She did. Craig sat next to her and put his arm around her and kissed her again. *I couldn't bear to watch. It was 9:15 in the morning and Craig's basic instincts were in control and knew what to do.*

***

At 11:15 a.m., Craig heard a knock at the door, followed by a voice.

"It's Thomas, Mr. Craig. Time to go to bingo."

Before Craig could speak, Thomas was in the room, standing at the foot of the bed. With shock and sadness, he looked down at Craig and Betty in bed and at their clothes that were strewn on the floor. Thomas was speechless. Pairing up was a common occurrence in memory care facilities. He had seen it before, but this seemed different. Craig and Betty were just lying there under the covers, staring up at Thomas.

"What do you want?" Craig asked.

Thomas paused for what seemed like an eternity but was really only a few seconds.

"Well, Mr. Craig and Miss Betty, it's time for prize bingo. Y'all always play before lunch on Thursdays."

Craig had reverted back to his normal state of confusion. He couldn't remember what had just happened with Betty, who had a peaceful look on her face.

Looking back at Thomas he said, "We're not playing today. We're taking a nap right now. Can you leave us alone please?"

Craig was often abrupt and harsh with Thomas, but not with this request. Thomas didn't know how to respond. He knew that the compliance answer was to leave and report the incident immediately to the charge nurse on duty. He also knew an investigation by the facility management team, a notification to the relatives, and a written plan for the future would soon follow. Thomas hated the idea of it all. He especially hated that Katy would be devastated and confused by what had transpired. Who wouldn't? However, Thomas had no choice. He had to report it.

Combining his compassion for the two of them with his sense of moral obligation, Thomas said, "Okay, Mr. Craig, you don't have to go to bingo if you don't want to. However, you do need to get up and get dressed soon because you are going home after lunch." He knew this would spark Craig's mind and cause a reaction.

As expected, Craig instantly perked up and smiled. "I am?"

"Yes. Katy is coming this afternoon. I'll go now so you and Miss Betty can get up from your nap and get dressed for lunch." Thomas turned and walked out of the room. As he reached the hallway, he sighed loudly, blowing breath out from deep in his lungs. He knew what he had to do next.

Heading for the nurses' station, Thomas passed through the main dining room and looked at the residents seated at the tables. They all had bingo cards and stacks of red and white chips. Shana had just finished placing the balls into the tumbler. Beside her was a basket of prizes—small stuffed animals, bags of cashews, candy bars, and other goodies. Shana told the residents to get ready, that the first ball would soon be picked. The metaphor of the random chaotic ball movement was not lost on Thomas.

At the nurses' station, he waited as the on-duty nurse, Sheila, divided medication into small plastic cups. He paused in the doorway until Sheila looked up.

"Hey, Thomas," she said. "What's up?"

"We've got a situation," Thomas answered in a matter-of-fact tone. "I just came from Mr. Craig's room. He and Miss Betty were in bed together, undressed."

Sheila looked uncomfortable and sighed. "Oh dear. Is this the first time?"

"As far as I know," he replied.

"Well, this sort of thing happens. I'll add it to my log and email Vanessa." Vanessa was the executive director of the entire facility. "Are they still in the room?"

"I think they're getting up soon and will likely be together for lunch."

ROUTINE CHAOS
Tritium (2005)

I t was 9:14 a.m. and Craig was at his desk looking at performance indicators. He loved these graphs and numbers. *If you can't measure it, you can't manage it,* he thought. These indicators covered everything from shipment timing to radiation events to bee stings.

Craig was the general manager of the Tritium Facilities at the Savannah River Site in Aiken, South Carolina. As contractors for the Department of Energy, Craig and his team's primary mission in running the facilities was to replace the tritium reservoirs for the U.S. nuclear weapons stockpile. Tritium, a highly unstable hydrogen isotope with two extra neutrons in the nucleus, is a primary component of thermonuclear weapons. He was proud of his job. He loved America and believed that nuclear weapons, for the most part, had kept the peace since World War II.

Craig looked up to see his operations manager, Stacy Ottly, in the doorway, looking rather alarmed. Craig promoted Stacy, who was in her early forties, to the job a year ago. She was grateful for the opportunity but felt she'd been promoted solely because of her gender. It was true that Craig's decision had been supported in part by performance indicators, multiple drivers for the advancement of women and minorities. Craig endorsed trying to improve Tritium's minority numbers whenever possible, but only when a minority candidate was as qualified as the non-minority candidate. Then, and only then, did he give preference to the minority. But Stacy was the best operations manager in the business; that was why he promoted her. She was head and shoulders above the other candidates. Despite his attempts to convince her, Stacy clung to her doubts.

"What is it?" Craig asked, concern on his face as he looked at her pale and panicked face.

"It's the control system," Stacy said as she walked into Craig's office. "We had a glove box release! We over-pressurized the system during loading. Something's bad wrong!"

Her heightened state made her southern drawl even more pronounced. "The system seems to be doin' whatever it wants," she added. "It's like it has a mind of its own!"

Craig's expression turned to stone. "Tell me more," he said. "Give me the facts."

"We were loading reservoirs. The shift manager—Billy—was entering the specifics, but the system kept changing the data. You know Billy's our best, at least for loading operations. He's been doing this for fifteen years; says he's never seen anything like it."

"Hold on a minute," Craig said. "Before we get to that, how are the facilities? Do we have a release? Is the gas contained? Is anyone hurt? Has there been an uptake?"

Craig's mind automatically switched to crisis mode. He had weathered many critical moments in his career and learned how to stifle his emotions, at least outwardly. The folks he counted on to fix the problems typically responded best to calm leadership. They also needed to see how concerned and involved he was in the process.

Craig's software package was composed of impressive logic and learning skills, consistently improving each year. It developed a unique style based on his experiences, both good and bad, that allowed him to make constant enhancements. In these situations, I just let it work its magic. I felt my job was to remind him to pray, which was a pretty easy task for me since Craig believed in the power of prayer, having witnessed the miracles God had performed in his life. As he talked with Stacy, I began to give him a nudge. His consciousness momentarily left her and went to the well.

Jesus, Craig thought, *help us with this, just like you always do.*

Throughout the facility, alarm sirens blared. Billy was in emergency response mode. He'd already called the Department of Energy facility representative, who was on his way to the control room, and was quickly rereading the emergency response procedure.

The alarms continued sounding because the sensors had monitored a massive amount of tritium in a glove box. Essentially, all the tritium operations happened in metal boxes with plexiglass windows. Those windows each had ports that contained long gloves the facility operators used to do their work. Everything happened with the use of these gloves. The boxes themselves were filled with nitrogen. Since tritium is a hydrogen gas and highly flammable, fires or explosions could occur and were a constant concern. The only thing worse than a tritium release was a fire. Thus, the nitrogen blanket within the boxes. Purification systems cleaned the nitrogen, removing any leaking tritium. The boxes were kept at a negative pressure, so if a leak occurred, it would be contained to the box and not enter the room. For now, it appeared that all the tritium released had stayed in the system and was contained.

Billy was now briefing the operations team and the DOE facility representative Terry Hidebound. The operators looked worried.

"How did this happen?" Hidebound asked.

"We're not sure yet," Billy answered, "but we will find out. Right now, we're focused on keeping the product in the system and cleaning the tritium from the box. So far, it looks like the system is working as designed, but there's a lot of tritium to remove. We are designed to handle it, but we are in design space now where we've never been before."

Hidebound took copious notes as the briefing went on. Terry had been a federal employee since he graduated from Clemson with a mechanical engineering degree. Rather slight in build and nearly bald, Terry was generally frustrated with his ability to affect what the contractor did because he was only to oversee and not direct the contractor. He felt fettered by his role. However, he'd have to apprise his boss and then his superiors in DC within the hour. His heart was pounding. He knew the suits in DC would ask limitless questions, most of which would be ridiculous.

Damn. Why did this have to happen on my watch? Hidebound thought. He had been a rep for nearly twenty years, taking part in numerous briefings, but he'd never been in one like this. What would follow would be painful. And then there would be the team DC assembled and sent down to do fact finding. It was going to be a nightmare, and one he wouldn't be able to escape.

***

Stacy looked at Craig, realizing she should have started with the status update that Craig clearly wanted.

"Well, the good news is that it looks to be contained," she said, the color in her face returning to normal. "Billy pulled the emergency procedure manual and is executing the response. I was down in the control room when it happened. The box was flooded, but it held. The purification system is up and running well. There have been no uptakes. We also haven't had any injuries, and no room alarms have sounded, at least not yet."

"All right, let's go to the facility," Craig said, grabbing his jacket from the back of his chair.

For a minute, Stacy toyed with the idea of asking Craig to wait, because the last thing Billy needed was Craig looking over his shoulder as he executed the emergency response. However, she knew Craig wouldn't be stopped. She nodded. "Okay," she said. "Let's go."

As they made their way out of the office building and into the courtyard, Craig grinned at Stacy. "Your hair's on fire; did you know that?"

"Yes, I do, sir," she responded with a forced smile.

Craig couldn't resist teasing her a bit; in his own weird way, he was trying to put her at ease.

"Where is the customer on this?" he asked, referring to the federal government.

"Hidebound was on his way when I came to tell you. I'm sure he will brief Dr. Oddlove as soon as he feels he has enough information."

Dr. Oddlove was the DOE counterpart to Craig.

"Maybe he already has," Stacy continued. "I'm sure Dr. Oddlove will want you there when he briefs headquarters."

"Oh yeah," Craig replied. "I'm not looking forward to that inquisition."

They made their way to the door of the facility, opened it, and walked toward the control room entrance. They then hurried down an immaculately clean hallway. The floors were tile and waxed weekly, so they shined. You could eat off them. The walls were freshly painted, the windows shined, and the halls were clear of trash. Tritium had the best reputation in the entire DOE Weapons Complex. No one disputed it. Their culture was one of disciplined operations, making them the best in the business, and Craig and virtually all of the Tritium employees were proud. He knew Tritium's reputation would help. This mishap wouldn't be like an event at Los Alamos or one of the cleanup sites where DC would be thinking, *"Here we go again."* No, DC would be surprised that Tritium had an emergency of this sort. Craig would use that reputation as he briefed DOE and participated in the investigation that was sure to come.

As they reached the door to the control room, Stacy asked, "Permission to enter?"

They were technically inside the control room, but a line marked the floor just in front of where they stood. There were two stanchions with a braided rope hanging between them, suspended above the line, to delineate the official control room. No one was to go beyond the line and rope without permission from the shift manager or whoever had been designated responsible for the control room.

Billy looked over his shoulder with a serious look. "Permission granted," he said.

Stacy worried that Craig's presence would make Billy a bit nervous, but she also knew that the situation promised to be even more intense as DOE and others showed up.

"Continue with your briefing, Billy. We're here to observe and won't bother you until you have time to brief us."

"Roger that," Billy said. "Glad to have you here, sir."

Craig listened intently as the briefing proceeded, knowing what to listen and watch for from his years of experience with other events. He looked for command and control by Billy. He listened for details that might give him ideas on the cause as well as feed for his soon-coming discussions with DOE. They would expect him to know every detail, so he would be prepared. His reputation depended on it.

Craig had a crisis formula. His software package had developed a fundamentals list that always worked. First, admit when something bad happens. Don't make excuses. There is nothing better than a well-placed admission, which mollified the customer's anger and created a more conducive atmosphere for discussion. There would be plenty of time to explain the hows and whys of the situation later. Start with an admission, then go to a well-laid-out recovery plan to instill customer confidence. Next, show progress in executing that plan, and then, and only then, offer a defense. Works every time. I was proud of and agreed with Craig's approach. I liked it, not only because it worked, but because it gave Craig credibility with the customer and his own organization. Others recognized Craig as a Christian who didn't lie, giving him a chance to softly witness about his faith, even in times of crisis. Yeah, I liked the strategy and believed God did too.

Suddenly, another loud alarm sounded, prompting Billy to halt the briefing and inspect the control panel over the operator's shoulder. The operator looked up. "Room alarm. There is tritium in that room, sir."

"Damn!" Billy exclaimed. "Pull the room alarm response procedure."

The operator pulled out the procedure. Billy already knew what it said, even as the operator read it aloud. He looked up at the three operators standing nearby.

"Jim, go look in the window of the room and report back. Do not—I repeat—do not open the door." Next, Billy turned to the operator with the room alarm procedure and asked in a commanding voice, "No hall alarms? No other alarms outside the room?"

"Roger that, sir. No alarms outside the room."

Craig noted that the operator demonstrated good repeat-back. When given a facility command or asked a question, the respondent should repeat back the question or command in a way that assured the asker that he understood it. While this was a pain during normal shift operations, during a real emergency it came naturally. It also came naturally when Craig was in the room. They knew he'd expect it.

The operator exited the control room and rushed to the alarming room. Through the window in the door, he saw the tritium alarm flashing inside. He also saw that the gloves were no longer inside the glove box, but outside and stiff, looking like a ghost was inside the box reaching out.

"Oh sh—!" the operator exclaimed. He knew what that meant; the box had over-pressurized and no longer had the negative pressure needed to keep the gloves in the box. Gas pressure on the inside of the box was pushing out.

The operator quickly returned to the control room and reported what he'd seen to Billy and the others. Billy then repeated the salient points and told the operator he'd already redirected the flow from the room. The problem now was the capacity of the gas purification systems to clean up the mess. The facility was designed to do just that but had never truly been tested.

There were several possible negative outcomes. Assuming it could be contained, if the gas processing system didn't work quickly enough or became overloaded, gas may need to be released to keep the rest of the facility from being contaminated. That would be a bad day.

Craig had been quiet thus far, but it was killing him. He was a bit of a control freak and wanted to get in the game. However, he also trusted Stacy and the operations crew, who knew the technical details much better than he did.

"How long before we will know how the purification system is doing?" Craig asked.

Stacy answered, "It's hard to tell, sir, but we have already begun trending its performance."

"I know," Craig said. "That was in the emergency briefing. I'm asking what you think."

Stacy knew what Craig had wanted but chose to give him the safe answer first.

"I really don't know, but we should have our answer within two or three hours. If things work as designed and the room holds whatever has leaked in, we should be fine. Well, fine from a release standpoint. Our lives are about to change for the next several months, I'm sure. Especially yours. I'm also worried about making shipments."

"Shipments are the least of our worries, Stacy. Just keep the plant clean and the gas inside it. If we do that, we'll be good."

He walked over to Terry Hidebound and said, "Are we doing okay on our response?"

Craig always showed respect to the facility reps. They could make his life hell, and he knew it. Besides that, they were a solid source of raw data on the facility's operations. They were there 24/7, collecting a ton of valuable data. However, he'd only get that information if they trusted him enough to share it.

Hidebound said, "Yes, good conduct of operations so far, but I'm perplexed about what I've heard. The response is spot-on, but how did this happen?"

The rep was already looking to the cause, which was natural because it would be the first question DC would ask. Hidebound loved to show his technical knowledge, especially to a big shot like Craig.

"I mean," Hidebound continued, "how the heck did the control system allow it to over-pressurize? The software is designed to keep that from happening. It went way over pressure. It wouldn't take Billy's command to limit it. It was as if it had a mind of its own. How the hell could that happen? I think it's a glitch in that new software we loaded last year. You know, the artificial intelligence package we tested and downloaded? I don't think you guys really understood how it worked. I mean, you could check all the parameters, but what about this so-called learning function? I never trusted it. I even put it in writing. I think that's it."

Craig knew exactly what the rep was saying and felt an immediate wave of concern come over him. He too had felt uneasy about the software, but the engineering department convinced him that it could be managed and would actually be safer and much more cost-effective than the previous system. The new software would learn from data it collected and recommend changes that would improve facility performance.

Wow, Craig thought. *This could be bad.*

I cued him, and he silently prayed for a safe recovery and quick fix to whatever had caused the leak.

"Thanks, Terry," Craig said. "I depend on your input, and I knew your concerns as we loaded the software. Engineering will be involved in the root cause evaluation, and I will make sure that there is no CYA by them if the software caused it. As I like to say, we will start with the truth and see where that takes us."

Hidebound smiled. He'd heard Craig say his "start with the truth" spiel before. Craig used the quote in crisis situations to put the troops at ease.

"When are you going to brief Dr. Oddlove?" Craig asked.

"In about fifteen minutes."

"Okay," said Craig. "I'll let you brief him in private; then I'm sure he will want to talk to me. Tell him I'll be up to see him as soon as I have enough information. Let him know I'll join him on the call to DC, if he wants me to."

"Will do," replied Hidebound.

They both turned their attention back to Billy and continued listening to the briefing. Billy was doing an excellent job, but the mood in the control room was somber.

"Permission to enter?" Craig heard from behind. It was Tom Palisade, Craig's engineering director.

"Granted," Billy said tersely.

Tom entered the control room and walked over to Craig and Stacy. Tom was five-foot-seven and balding and had a master's degree in engineering from Alabama. Though brilliant, Tom was often defensive. His lack of a sense of humor was amplified by his social awkwardness.

"Damn," he said to Craig. "I can't believe this happened."

Tom had been briefed by one of his engineers who'd been in the facility when the incident occurred.

"How did the system over-pressurize?" Tom asked rhetorically.

Craig couldn't let the question go, especially since Hidebound was listening.

"You tell me," Craig responded.

"I sure don't know right now, but I will find out," Tom answered, worry clear in his voice.

Stacy spoke up. "We are trending gas purification performance, Tom, and so far, so good."

"Great. We are designed for just this kind of accident, but I never wanted a real test."

"Tell me about it," Stacy replied.

"You're right to focus on purification, Stacy," Tom added. "If it works, we will be all right."

"Did you know the event room is contaminated?" she asked Tom.

"No, I didn't, but it doesn't surprise me. That's too much gas for that glove box. Did we reconfigure the room air?" he asked, already fully aware of the answer but needing Craig to know that he understood just what the facility required.

"Yes, of course," said Stacy.

Craig caught it all but said nothing. He was focused on the gas purification graphics displayed on Billy's screen.

Billy turned to the operator who had checked the room. "Please go back to the event room and look at the gloves. See if there's any difference in their appearance. The glove box pressure is beginning to go down, and the gloves should not be at attention anymore."

"Yes, sir," he responded. "Going back to the event room to check glove status."

As the operator prepared to leave the control room, Craig tried to remember his name but couldn't. He was a great auxiliary operator, and Craig had spent several back-shifts in the facility with him, but now he couldn't even recall his name.

Hmm, Craig thought. *That's odd. I'm great with names; why can't I remember his? Oh well, guess I'm getting old.* But Craig was just sixty-two, and his memory had always been sharp.

It puzzled him, and me too, a bit. It was another inkling of the trouble to come.

Hidebound got up at the same time the operator did. "I'll go with you," he said. Looking at Craig, he added, "I'm going to have a look at the room and then head over to see Dr. Oddlove."

"Tell him I'll be there in forty minutes. Is that enough time for you to brief him?"

"Yes, plenty. See you then."

Craig waited a few minutes before saying to Stacy, "I'm going up to my office. Work with Tom to get all the relevant details you think we'll need to brief the doctor."

"Yes, sir," Stacy replied.

"I want you to go with me, Stacy. I'll take the lead, but you can fill in the technical details."

"Of course."

"Should I be there too?" Tom asked.

"No. I don't want to get into speculation on the call; I just need pure status and facts—only the things that we know for certain. If you come, they will immediately go to the engineering why. I need to hold that off until we figure this out, and we can do that best if engineering isn't there. I'll try to convince Dr. Oddlove that we should take the same tact for the headquarters call. If I'm not successful, I'll page you."

"Yes, sir," Tom responded.

Craig continued, "Hidebound is already making comments about the software upgrade being part of the cause. Of course, he can't possibly know that, but he was the thorn in our flesh that made the upgrade more difficult. I just hope he's wrong."

"Oh no, sir. The software didn't cause it," Tom responded.

Craig's blood pressure spiked, and it took everything he and I had to control an outburst.

Craig looked sternly at Tom. "I'm going to pretend I didn't hear that, Tom. There is no way you could possibly know that. No way. As always, I want a totally unbiased assessment of the facts, not some CYA from engineering. Got it?"

Tom's face turned the same color as the flashing red lights on the control panel.

"Yes, sir," he responded. "As you always say, we will start with the truth and see where that takes us. I just don't think—" He stopped himself mid-sentence as he caught Craig's glare. "Sorry, sir, you can count on me to uncover the truth."

"I hope that's true," Craig replied with a hardened gaze.

Craig then turned and left the control room. He was furious with Tom, but he controlled himself. He knew he could count on Stacy to get to the bottom of it and watch Tom for defensiveness.

Stacy had heard the discussion and knew exactly her delicate predicament. She was not the kind of person to use this to burn Tom. She would do the right thing, though, and that could be tough.

As Craig made his way through the courtyard toward his office, his mind fired wildly. He bounced from thought to thought. He wanted to focus on his upcoming meeting with Dr. Oddlove and the call to HQ, but he was having a hard time focusing on any one given topic.

I should go to my office and pray, Craig thought.

I had directed that thought, and it took.

When Craig got to his office, he closed the door and sat down. *Jesus, I need your help,* he began. *I'm not sure how all this happened or why. I just know I need your Holy Spirit now to bring me clarity and peace as we address this situation. Please let the gas be contained. I need you, Jesus.*

Pulling out his notepad, Craig began feverishly writing the notes for his briefing. He needed to keep DOE focused on the facility and the recovery and use his "best in the complex" status to keep them from going berserk. Be humble, yet assuring, and convey that he "had this" and that there would be a happy, safe ending. Deflect the *why* questions until later. That may take some forcefulness, but if he was open and honest with what he knew, they would know there was no way *why* could possibly be answered yet. However, he was sure he would be pressed to give a time when the *why* could be answered.

The knock at the door let him know time was up. Notepad in hand, Craig greeted Stacy.

"Ready? Let's go brief the customer."

***

Stacy and Craig entered the DOE building and walked to Dr. Oddlove's office. The building was a normal government structure. The halls were straight, narrow, and normally very quiet. However, now the office had been turned into a beehive of noise; everyone inside was talking about the incident. A sullen-faced Craig stood in the doorway.

"Come in," Dr. Oddlove said expressionlessly.

Dr. Oddlove was a great customer. He too was in his early sixties and had been a fed his whole career, working his way up the ladder to the prestigious level he now held. He had achieved it through his natural intelligence as well as his willingness to take an occasional risk and make hard decisions—traits that set him apart in the federal government. Just shy of six-foot-two and weighing 160 pounds, Oddlove wore a button-down collared dress shirt and loose-fitting dress slacks. He was thin but looked to be in great shape with his still-brown, buzz-cut hair. He and Craig were more than working counterparts; they were friends. There was a deep trust and respect between them, enhanced by their common value system, though Dr. Oddlove was agnostic. They had been through much together. And while they did not see each other socially, they had a working knowledge of each other's families.

Craig and Stacy joined Oddlove and Hidebound at the conference table.

"Wow. Quite a morning," Dr. Oddlove began. "Needed to get my blood pressure up this morning did you, Craig?"

Craig smiled and proceeded to go through all that was known about the event so far. Dr. Oddlove let him finish, though Hidebound had already covered it all. When he finished, Craig turned it over to Stacy. "I'll let Stacy give you some technical data, as she's just come from the control room."

Stacy passed copies around to everyone at the table and began her briefing. "These are graphs of the pressure rise and fall of the glove box, gas purification performance, and the activity outside the glove box in the event room," she began, and then went on to explain in great detail why the pressure was what it was. Apparently, it was a very significant dump to the glove box. "We were ramping up the system and pressurizing when the system kept going beyond the set point. That much we know. The operator recognized it and immediately shut off the gas feed, but it was too late. Something failed inside the box. We aren't sure if it was the feed system or something else."

Commanding their full attention, she continued, "The graph showing the activity in the room tells a reasonably good story. There is a small spike and then it stabilizes and begins to fall. That was when we reconfigured the room ventilation per our emergency response procedure to draw more air from the event room. There has been no leak outside the room. The graph of the purification system shows that it is working as designed. However, it is close to capacity. As long as it continues to work well, we could be back to normal in less than a week. We are making plans now to enter the event room. We will, of course, be in closed-air breathing. We are developing parameters to show us when it will be safe, which naturally will be when we have regained negative glove box pressure and the room is near background radioactivity again. We will know more by tonight."

Stacy always did an exceptional job. Dr. Oddlove and Hidebound both respected her.

"What do you think happened?" Dr. Oddlove asked.

Both Craig and Stacy knew the question was coming and had rehearsed an answer.

"I don't know, sir," Stacy replied. "I truly don't know, but I'm working with Tom to figure it out. We are selecting a root cause analysis team as we speak, and they will begin collecting data tomorrow."

"Yes, Doctor, and our primary focus is recovering the facility," Craig added. "I know headquarters will want to know cause as soon as possible, and we will find out as soon as possible. But I can't let that distract us from our facility focus. We need to let headquarters know that we will keep them informed, though it may take a while."

"I agree," said Dr. Oddlove. He trusted Craig's judgment, as did headquarters. However, if the causal analysis took too long, that trust would be tried.

Hidebound remained quiet throughout the briefing, but Craig was certain he had already spoken to Dr. Oddlove about his suspicions concerning the AI software. Craig felt Hidebound wanted to demonstrate that he was smarter, or at least as smart as they were. Proving that he had warned the contractor before the incident would definitely make Terry's light shine brighter. If he was right and HQ knew it, Terry's stock would rise immeasurably. Craig left it alone for the moment. He would discuss it one-on-one with Dr. Oddlove once he had more information.

Stacy was shifting gears in her presentation. "The first job of the analysis team will be to develop a timeline of events. That will shed crucial light on the event, and we should be able to brief you on it tomorrow."

Nicely done, Craig thought. *That will be something I add to my HQ discussion.* It would give him a little more time before he had to provide specifics. Craig knew that you didn't give DC any information without first presenting a caveat. If you told them particulars that they then passed on to their bosses, and then you changed the facts, you created a bad situation in DC. The secretary would be briefed on this one, and the last thing Craig needed was to go back a second time to the secretary to change the intelligence.

"Okay," Dr. Oddlove said. "I think I'm good for now. I'll set up a call with headquarters later today. Craig, I'd like for you to lead the briefing, but Stacy is certainly welcome to be there."

"Yes, sir," Craig responded. "Just give me a call. Claire will come and get me if I'm not at my desk."

At this, Craig and Stacy got up and left Dr. Oddlove's office. Stacy went back to the control room, and Craig returned to his office to update Claire, his executive assistant.

"Claire, Dr. Oddlove will be calling sometime today to let me know when we'll be briefing DC," said Craig, noticing how Claire's dark hair curled gently around her shoulders. Claire was thirty-five years old and a knockout.

"Yes, sir. Is everything okay?"

"I guess it is," Craig replied. "As long as the gas purification system works, we will be fine."

Craig had selected Claire as his assistant a year ago. She was quite competent at her job, but her looks were a distraction. She was not a conservative dresser either, which at times caused Craig to steal glances whenever he was sure he could get away with it.

I tried to prevent Craig from hiring her. I knew it could get ugly. However, if I'm honest, I didn't try too hard. She was a beauty, and I liked looking at her too.

WHO'S WHO
Fall Leaves (2012)

At a little past noon, Craig and Betty were out of bed and walking together toward the dining room. And although their faces still wore the same blank stares as usual, an aura of tranquility surrounded them. They both had a perception that a missing puzzle piece in their lives had been put back into place. They couldn't completely make sense of what they were feeling, but both felt as if something broken had been repaired. They were at peace with whatever they were feeling.

I was confused by it all, but in a strange way I also felt relieved.

Sitting down together, Craig stared at Betty, inwardly acknowledging his affection for her; affection that made him feel odd and comforted simultaneously. He wasn't exactly sure what to make of it, especially since he had no recollection of their time together in bed. Not long after they chose seats at the table, Shana sat plates down in front of them.

"Y'all want coffee, soda, or just water with your lunch?" she asked. Her question was answered with blank stares. She walked away and came back with two glasses of water.

"Here you go," she said with a smile, then walked back to the counter area to prepare additional lunch plates.

As Betty and Craig ate their lunches in silence, Thomas approached them.

"Hey, Miss Betty and Mr. Craig, I see y'all finished your nap. You missed an exciting game of bingo. Miss Olga won three times in a row."

"What nap?" a perplexed Craig asked.

Thomas was digging for more information to help him develop a plan that would prevent future "naps." He also wanted to figure out the best way to tell Katy.

I saw helplessness and sadness fill Thomas's eyes as he was again reminded of the reality of the residents' lives in this facility. Craig's short-term memory was now at less than a few minutes; no recall, except for occasional patches of long term. Comments about Cleveland, Aiken, and especially Katy prompted Craig to have a genuine recollection, but quizzing him about something from just two minutes ago would draw only a blank stare or defensive reply.

"Never mind," Thomas said with a sigh. "Enjoy your lunch." He then walked back to the nurses' station.

Sheila had just finished her meds distribution and was reading an email from Vanessa. The executive director's response to the apparent affair between Craig and Betty was what Sheila expected. Vanessa had given her the formal, corporate response; Sheila respected her, but Vanessa completely toed the company line.

"Standard response," Sheila told Thomas. "Totally compliant." Then she read it aloud to him.

Thanks for the heads-up, Sheila. As you know, these situations are common in our industry. In fact, we have had more than one at Marietta Fall Leaves. There is nothing that can or should be done by you or the facility staff to either prevent or encourage this behavior, except to assure that there has been no coercive or abusive behavior associated with said event. Moving forward, you should ask Thomas, since he is most familiar with the two individuals involved, to perform an unobtrusive investigation to assure nothing coercive or abusive has happened. Please give me his input when he's rendered an opinion. I would like it within twenty-four hours, if at all possible. Upon receiving his input, I will notify the next of kin.

"Yeah, that's about what I expected," Thomas said. "Tell her I've seen no coercive or abusive behavior." Thomas truly had no evidence of misconduct, but he would be on the lookout for red flags. He knew Craig had been a solid Christian man, a man of integrity. However, Thomas also knew that now there were two distinctly different Craigs. Unfortunately, that made the unthinkable a possibility.

Thomas was already beginning to play out scenarios in his mind of informing Katy, which caused a deep and profound sadness to descend on him. *Help me, Jesus*, he prayed silently, as he stood next to Sheila. *Help me deal with this. Lord, help me have the right words for Katy so she won't go to pieces; and finally, Lord, help Mr. Craig and Miss Betty to stop this and just be friends.*

After finishing his prayer, he asked Sheila to include in her correspondence with Vanessa his request to be the one to break the news to Katy. Thomas wanted to take on the task himself so he could help Katy deal with the pain and confusion and devise a path forward.

Sheila said, "Sure, I will. However, I doubt she'll let you. It's our policy to send a formal notification to the family, and Vanessa seldom, if ever, strays from policy."

"You're right, Sheila, but still ask. Also, please ask Vanessa to let us know when she's sent the notification if she doesn't let me tell her."

"I will, Thomas," she replied.

* * *

Back at their table, Craig and Betty had finished lunch and were sitting quietly. Craig looked tenderly at Betty and said, "You're certainly a beautiful woman."

Looking down at her empty plate, Betty blushed and said, "Thank you."

While Shana removed their dirty dishes, Craig and Betty stood up and walked back to Craig's room as if they had been together since they were teenagers. If one didn't know better, one would think they had been married for years. They entered Craig's room; Betty sat on the bed and Craig sank into his recliner, picked up the remote control, and turned on the TV. An infomercial for cutlery blared. They both stared at the screen and said nothing.

I was confused. What was happening? They were acting like a couple, which left me troubled. Craig was a Christian. How could he just sleep with this woman? In vain, I tried to arouse memories of Anne. I tried to remind him of his wedding ceremony, of Katy's birth, of their trips together as a family. It was useless. Nothing fired. Craig just sat there watching the guy tell him how he could get knives that could cut steel and still slice a tomato. He was on autopilot.

At 6:10 in the evening, Katy pulled into her driveway. She had been in court most of the day after leaving Fall Leaves.

"Hey, babe," Mark called out as Katy walked into their house. He was mixing a salad as he smiled at her.

Mark sold real estate and had a much more flexible schedule than Katy. He usually got home before their daughter did and frequently prepared dinner. He was a dedicated, loyal, and hard-working man. His whole life revolved around his family. He was handsome with dark hair he combed straight back, and, though humble, he could turn on the charm—which made him a great salesman.

"Hey, honey," Katy replied. "What's for dinner?"

"Making a salad and reheating chicken from yesterday to add to it. Sorry, but I didn't get home until about a half hour ago. Sold one today and had to stay with my clients to keep them happy."

"Awesome! Nice house?"

"Yes," Mark replied. "A twenty-year-old place off Peachtree. Man, the market is good right now."

"Is Cameron home?"

"Just got back from soccer practice a few minutes ago. She's in her room."

Remembering she hadn't checked her personal email in hours, Katy glanced at her phone as she leaned against the kitchen counter. She only had three messages, one of which was from Fall Leaves. It read:

Mrs. Jarred,

I hope this writing finds you well. I am reaching out to inform you of a situation that has arisen at Marietta Fall Leaves concerning your father. It seems one of our caregivers witnessed Craig in bed with another resident of our facility, both in a state of undress. We have conducted an initial assessment, and there appears to be no evidence of coercive or abusive behavior. It is our policy to neither encourage nor discourage this type of behavior. As always, we want what is best for our residents and their families. At your convenience, please contact us concerning this matter so that we can assure everyone's best interests are served.

Thank you for your continued support in these matters,
Vanessa Adhere, Executive Director

Katy laid her phone on the table and sat down in a nearby chair. She was devastated. She had the feeling of having seen a puppy run over in the street. Mark looked up from the salad preparation and saw her face.

"What is it, honey? What's wrong?"

"Oh my God! Dad is sleeping with another woman!" She began to tear up, feeling a combination of shock, sadness, anger, and helplessness.

"What?" said Mark. "I certainly didn't see that coming. Do we know who it is?"

"No, they're probably prohibited from putting that in writing. Fall Leaves is a compliance prison. The email reads like a deposition notice, for crying out loud. The only real person there is Thomas. The rest are compliance robots." While she knew that wasn't totally true, Katy was upset and needed to vent.

"What do we do?" Mark asked.

"I honestly don't have a clue," Katy answered. "Dad is going from bad to worse. He is crude and mean, and now this—an affair! Who is he?" she asked rhetorically.

"This is not your dad," Mark replied. "It's someone else. He loved your mother more than himself, and it showed. He never even noticed other women except to help them. I'm not sure who this is, but it's not your dad."

Mark knew how to calm Katy down during stressful times.

"I know," Katy replied solemnly as she hit the contact number for Fall Leaves. After five rings, the call was answered by the nurses' station since the receptionist had gone for the day.

"Marietta Fall Leaves. This is Sheila. How can I help you?"

"Hi, Sheila. This is Katy Jarred."

"Oh hi, Katy. I guess you got the email from Vanessa?"

"I just did," Katy responded, fighting back tears that had welled up once again. "What happened?"

"Well, Thomas went into your father's room this morning and found him in bed with another resident."

"Which resident?" Katy asked.

"Um, we really are only supposed to discuss this with you in person, but I guess it wouldn't hurt to tell you. It was Miss Betty. You know Betty, don't you? Your dad often eats at the same table with her."

"I do," Katy replied. "How can I find out more?"

"Why don't you come down here so we can discuss everything. Our shift is ending soon. Thomas and I are leaving at seven. Can we do it tomorrow? Perhaps before you go to work, or after you get off?"

Katy began to think. There was no way she could sleep tonight without knowing more. "If I leave my house now, I can be there by seven. Is there any way you could wait until I get there?" Katy asked.

"I really can't stay tonight, Katy. I'm just now beginning my turnover."

"How about Thomas? Can I talk to him, please?"

"I suppose so; let me see if I can find him." Sheila put the receiver down and stuck her head out of her office. Thomas was standing next to the counter helping put away dirty dinner dishes.

"Thomas, can you come here for a minute?"

Thomas put the plate in his hand on the cart and walked over to Sheila.

"It's Katy Jarred. Can you speak to her?"

"Sure," Thomas said and picked up the receiver.

"Hey, Katy. This is Thomas." His voice was sincere. Normally if he was talking to Katy, he would be in the best of moods. Not this time; he knew what this call was about.

"Hey, Thomas. Wow, I just read the email from Vanessa. What an email. What's going on there?"

"Well, I found Mr. Craig and Miss Betty undressed in bed this morning. I had no choice but to report it. I wanted to tell you myself in person, but policy prohibited it. But I'd like to talk you through it and discuss what we should do from here."

"Me too," Katy replied. "I can be there in twenty minutes, but I know you get off soon."

"Oh, don't worry about that. If you want to come now, then come. I'll stay here until we talk it through and you feel at peace about what we should do."

"Thank you so much," Katy said with tears streaming down her cheeks. "I'll see you soon."

***

At a few minutes past seven, Katy took the elevator to the second floor, walked to the door, and entered her code. As she passed the nurses' station, she spied Thomas seated in one of the dining room chairs waiting for her.

"Hey, Katy. You doing okay?"

"No, not really."

They had the room to themselves. Katy took a seat across from Thomas and asked him to tell her everything.

"Of course. You should know that, as far as I can tell, today was the first time this occurred—I asked around before I submitted my report. So, after you left this morning, your dad and Miss Betty finished eating and then went to his room. I didn't see it, but Shana did. I went to his room just after eleven to remind him about prize bingo. He always plays and loves to win those bags of chocolates and cookies. I go into the room, and there they are—in bed. Their clothes off, at least the outer layers."

"Were they embracing?" Katy asked.

"No, they were just lying on their backs, staring at the ceiling."

"Do you think anything happened?" Katy asked shyly.

"I really don't know, Katy. I don't."

"Sorry to ask you that, Thomas. It really wasn't appropriate, but I had to."

"I understand, Katy. Don't worry about it."

Katy sat rubbing her forehead in silence. After about a minute, she began to cry.

"Thomas, this isn't my dad. He was always such a good man. He loved my mother and me. He went to church. He didn't curse. I know he never had an affair. He loved us and God too much. Now, he is someone else. He's sleeping with a stranger. I don't understand how this could happen. I just don't know who he is anymore."

"I know. I struggle with it too. Not just for Mr. Craig, but for others here as well. How can a person change so much? I get how you can become forgetful as you age and your brain changes, but a total personality change makes no sense to me."

"I believe my dad still loves God and is a Christian, but where is he and who is this new dad? I can't take it!"

Thomas reached across the table and put his hands on top of Katy's as she continued to cry.

"Is it okay if I pray?"

Katy nodded and smiled through her tears.

"Jesus, we love you and come to you tonight with heavy hearts. We know that you are our Lord and Savior, and we need you now. We don't understand why this has happened or why Mr. Craig is like he is or why Miss Betty is like she is. We just know that this isn't right, and we pray for your intervention. Please, somehow let this stop and give us back the old Mr. Craig. Lord, give us your guidance and direction on how to handle this as well as comfort and strength to go through it. Bless Katy and give her peace. I pray in Jesus's name, amen."

Katy wiped the tears from her cheeks. "What do we do now?"

"Let's start with the established boundaries and go from there. The facility will not let us restrict the residents in any way. That's actually the law, as I'm sure you know."

Katy nodded.

"We can't even tell them not to do it unless we believe there is some sort of coercion or abuse occurring. I've seen no indication of that. It just seems almost natural. Now, of course, you can do whatever seems right to you, and I want you to know that I will help you however I can. You know I don't always follow the policies. I try and do what's best for the residents."

"I know you do, Thomas. It's who you are. Your job is a ministry, and I hope you know how much I appreciate you. Do you think this was just a one-time thing, or do you think it will happen again?"

Thomas stared at Katy for a few seconds, then with a somber face said, "It will continue."

"How do you know that?"

"Because they are sleeping together right now. Miss Betty took some of her things into Mr. Craig's room after dinner. They changed into their pajamas and are in there now watching TV in bed. I just left them before you came in."

"Wow," Katy sighed. "Should I go in and talk to them? What do I do, Thomas?"

Thomas thought for a minute and then said, "Well, if you think it's best, of course you should. However, you might want to wait until tomorrow morning. You know they are much better in the morning. Tonight, they are both confused and might have a worse response than tomorrow. I mean, unless you want to try and separate them now. You can if you want, but I wouldn't advise it. It could get ugly quick. You know how Mr. Craig gets when he's angry. It might be better to wait." Thomas ran his hand over his head and sighed.

"I can have the nurse give him his meds before breakfast tomorrow morning," he continued. "That way, you could be here by 7:30 and talk to them. Craig is usually good in the morning, especially after his meds. And if something has happened between them, it has already happened. But, of course, it's up to you."

Katy thought for a moment. "You're right, Thomas. If I go in there now, it could get ugly. Also, I need to prepare myself for it. I don't want to go to pieces, and I don't even know what I should say. I'll go home now, pray, and think it through. I'll come back tomorrow morning, hopefully better prepared."

"Sounds right, Katy," Thomas replied. "I will be praying too. We will get through this. It's just another challenge that God will solve."

"Thank you, Thomas. I'll see you tomorrow," Katy said as she got up and walked to the elevator.

***

Meanwhile, Craig and Betty lay silently in bed, listlessly watching a George Foreman grill infomercial. Thoughts rolled around in their minds. Their expressions were peaceful, but uncertain.

Craig looked over at Betty and asked, "Are you okay?"

"Yes, I am. I'm fine. Can I get you something?" she asked Craig out of instinct. There was obviously nothing she could get, but it was just her memory kicking in for a second. She used to lay in bed with her husband and ask him the same question. Though perhaps she should have kicked him out of bed for his behavior, she had loved her husband and tolerated his antics.

"No, thanks," Craig said as he scooted over closer to Betty. He liked the feel of her warm body. It brought back memories to him as well, though he couldn't really make sense of them. He just knew he liked what she felt like. It brought a peace over him. Silence ensued and the infomercial played on.

I was confused by all of this. I was no longer able to control Craig; he was on autopilot ninety-nine percent of the time. Okay, I got that. But what Craig was doing seemed wrong to me. I mean, Craig always loved having sex, and I did too, but he was always faithful to Anne. If I was still in charge, this would never have happened. It's a disgrace to Anne's memory. And then there's Katy. It was bad enough that she knew how Craig cussed and said terrible things to Thomas. Now this. I'd slap him if I could.

It was 5:30 a.m. and Katy had been up for half an hour. She'd already made a cup of coffee and was sitting quietly in her favorite chair. Thoughts of her dad in bed with another woman dominated her attention and made her sad. She came home last night and briefly discussed the situation with Mark. Before going to bed, the two of them had prayed for guidance. To her surprise, when she awoke, she realized that she had gone right to sleep and had slept well. But now it was time to face the issue. As usual, Katy woke early so she'd have a few minutes alone with just her thoughts and coffee, followed by a brief devotion. This morning's prayer time was unfocused. Her mind kept drifting back to her dad.

She put her coffee down and reached for her Bible. Whenever she had difficulty praying, she'd read a chapter or two of scripture. Though she was a driven, goal-oriented person, Katy wasn't one to read the Bible on a schedule or plan. She preferred slowly reading it, meditating and praying as she went. Her last reading had been from the Old Testament, and she opened her Bible to where she'd left off, 1 Kings 1: 1–4. It read:

> When King David was very old, he could not keep warm even when they put covers over him. So his attendants said to him, "Let us look for a young virgin to serve the king and take care of him. She can lie beside him so that our lord the king may keep warm." Then they searched throughout Israel for a beautiful young woman and found Abishag, a Shunammite, and brought her to the king. The woman was very beautiful; she took care of the king and waited on him, but the king had no sexual relations with her.

In shock, Katy sat her Bible down and looked up to her ceiling. "Wow!" she said aloud. "Wow."

A stream of thoughts and emotions flowed through her mind like a turbulent river. She thought of how politically incorrect this was—a beautiful woman forced to sleep with an old man. Really? This was male chauvinism at its finest. She then thought of King David, whom she'd always loved reading about and studying. He was a "bad dude." A mighty warrior with a heart for God. And it was clear that God loved him, because David had always sought Him. God was always faithful to forgive David despite his flaws and missteps, like the Bathsheba affair. Katy wanted to meet David in Heaven. He had to be something special.

She then began to pray, asking God to lead her. She asked God if this scripture was meant for her to read and take to heart. As she was praying, a peace came over her. It was that peace that she got when she felt God's presence. She had always been taught that the peace of God was supernatural. Maybe it was and maybe it wasn't, but either way, she felt it now.

She smiled and again said aloud, "Wow."

***

At 6:45 a.m., Katy was backing out of her driveway, headed for Fall Leaves after making a quick breakfast for Mark and Cameron. She didn't go into any detail with Mark except to say that she had a plan and that she felt good about it. When Mark pressed for details, Katy told him they'd discuss it that evening, then she kissed him goodbye and headed out the door.

Katy hurried into her car and stopped at a coffee shop, where she ordered three coffees and two Danish pastries. Once at Fall Leaves, Katy took the coffees and pastries to the Emerald floor and went straight to Craig's room. She put the drink tray on the floor and knocked on the door. She waited and then knocked again. Finally, she heard Craig say, "Who is it?"

"It's me, Dad. It's Katy," she said as she picked up the coffees and entered the room.

There lay Craig and Betty, their clothes folded neatly at the foot of the bed. Only their heads were outside the covers. Craig and Betty smiled.

"Hey there pretty, young, and brilliant daughter of mine," Craig said. "Whatcha got there?"

"I brought a coffee and a Danish for both you and Betty."

"Who?" Craig asked.

"Betty, the young lady next to you."

"Oh. I love a Danish and coffee."

"I know, Dad. I know," Katy replied. "Why don't you and Betty get up and get dressed? You can drink your coffee while you're getting ready. I'll wait outside, and then come back in when you're dressed. We can talk while you finish your coffee and Danish."

Craig smiled at Katy. "Okay, Katy. That's great. I love coffee and Danish, and you're my best daughter."

As Katy left the room, she locked eyes with Thomas, who was walking down the hall. He looked puzzled.

"Were you in there with them just now?" he asked.

"I was."

"Are you okay?"

"Yes, Thomas, I am. I prayed last night and again this morning, and I somehow have a sense of peace about all this. It's as if the Holy Spirit, our Comforter, comforted me. I know that sounds like a cliché, but it's real."

"I know it is," agreed Thomas. "Praise God. Tell me more."

Katy recounted her experience during her morning devotional time. She told Thomas of the scripture she had read about King David.

"I don't know if it's coincidental that I read that scripture this morning, but it sure helped me."

"That's amazing," said Thomas. "I know God gave you that scripture. No way that was coincidental. Just so you know, Miss Betty and your dad both seem very peaceful. I mean, Mr. Craig has been so pleasant, not that he wasn't before," Thomas added, fearing Katy would feel he was complaining about her father.

Katy smiled and said, "No need to backtrack, Thomas. I know how my dad can be at times. It really isn't him, and you know that."

"I'm so glad that you recognize that too," Thomas said.

"I'm letting them get dressed, and then I'm going to go in there and drink my coffee with them. I hope that's okay."

"Of course it is, Katy. You and your visit this morning have been on my mind ever since we talked last night. Thank you for being so strong. It has made my day. You the woman, Katy!"

Katy smiled. "Well, I'm going into the breach. Pray for me again, Thomas," she said as she opened the door and entered her dad's room.

Craig and Betty were seated together on the love seat with their pastries on their laps. They were quietly eating and sipping coffee. Katy took a seat in the recliner and looked at the new couple. Both were well dressed since Katy always made sure that Craig had nice clothes, and Betty's son Levi did the same for her. However, Betty and Craig both had severe bedhead. Betty had a pronounced flat spot in the back, and Craig's combover was hanging down to his left ear. Katy asked if they had slept well. They both smiled and said "yes" in unison.

I was shocked. I couldn't believe how calmly Katy was behaving. I mean, seeing her dad in bed with another woman had to be difficult for her. The whole thing was killing me. I had always been able to pretty much keep Craig on track. Well, we did have our times, if I'm honest. The truth is, I allowed Craig to do things I knew were wrong because I also liked to do them. But I knew that it was me who allowed, or at least facilitated, those behaviors. I always knew we would ultimately straighten up and that God would be there to forgive us. But I had no hand in this. I hadn't wanted to sleep with Betty. At least I don't think so. My biggest mission now was to keep him calm so that it brought as little pain as possible to Katy, Thomas, and others. If this romance with Betty helped somehow, maybe it wasn't so bad. I know that God works in mysterious ways, but this was like an Alfred Hitchcock movie. I guess I just hang on, look for moments of connection with Craig, and try to do some good.

THE SLIPPERY SLOPE
Tritium (2005)

At 1:30 p.m. Craig was at his desk compiling the facts and preparing for the DC call when Claire interrupted him.

"Dr. Oddlove's assistant just contacted me. The call with Washington is in fifteen minutes. Do you need my help with anything?" she asked.

"No, thanks. I'm as ready as I'm gonna be. Please page Stacy and have her meet me at his office."

"Yes, sir," she responded, as he picked up the papers from his desk, pounded them into a neat pile, put them in his planner, and headed for the door.

He arrived at Dr. Oddlove's office, walked in unceremoniously, and took a place at the conference table. Hidebound was already there.

"Is Stacy coming?" Hidebound asked.

"She's on her way," Craig answered.

"Okay, Craig," Dr. Oddlove began. "I will start the call with a status of where we are and then turn it over to you. You can ask Stacy to jump in whenever you feel is best to answer questions and fill in technical gaps. We'll let the contractor handle this one," he added with a wry smile.

"Yes, sir," Craig responded with a similar smile. "As it should be."

Craig knew that he and his company were responsible for the current situation, and he wasn't trying to avoid accountability. His job was to credit the customer for all good things they did while accepting the blame himself for the bad stuff. This philosophy played a large role in his success. From time to time, staff members would complain about the "dumb customer," prompting an immediate reprimand from Craig. He would remind them that they were all blessed to have their jobs—jobs that helped put all their children, including Katy, through college. No besmirching the customer. Period.

Craig looked up as Stacy entered the room. "Sorry, am I late?"

"No, Stacy, right on time as always. Please have a seat. Dr. Oddlove will start the call, then I will take over. I'll cue you if I need help. Of course, the customer can chime in whenever they want; it's their party," Craig said with a smile.

Dr. Oddlove jumped in. "Well, this one may be your party."

Craig had said the last part for the benefit of Hidebound, certain that he had apprised Dr. Oddlove on the AI error potential. Craig knew that both Dr. Oddlove and Hidebound could harp on the issue during the call; it was definitely their prerogative. However, he hoped they would not, at least not until he had time to investigate it himself.

The call began with Dr. Oddlove giving a short summary of what had already been reported. Then it was Craig's turn.

"Unfortunately, I won't be able to tell you much more than what Dr. Oddlove said, except that we have already begun our investigation, parallel with our recovery. Be assured, I won't let the investigation in any way hamper the recovery. The facility has performed as designed, and I am very thankful for that. We never wanted to be here, but this is a credible accident in our safety basis. I don't say that to insinuate that it was expected or as a

CYA. It was not. We will get to the bottom of how and why it happened, and I will not sugarcoat the findings."

Craig was relying on his reputation as a straight shooter as a bargaining chip with DC. He knew they trusted him, which he used to put them at ease. It seemed to work.

Dr. Oddlove's boss, who went by NA-1—DOE jargon for the number-one position in Dr. Oddlove's chain of command—was on the line. He said, "I know you will, Craig. What are the chances for a release of some sort?"

"Great question," Craig replied. "That is our main concern. As long as the gas purification system performs as designed, we should be fine. We will do everything in our power to avoid a release. We can't go back in time to when an elemental release was no big deal. The public won't understand that a substantial release today was a routine event twenty years ago. They won't be forgiving. I get it."

"Exactly right," NA-1 responded. "Keep the gas off the plants."

"Roger that," Craig agreed.

As the conversation continued, Craig had trouble focusing, which surprised him, especially during an important meeting with the customer. He kept harking back to a joke an engineer once told him during one of their back-shift all-nighters. The engineer was with Craig most of the night going over logs, answering questions, and monitoring glove boxes. The atmosphere had become relaxed and friendly as the night wore on. As Craig and the engineer looked at the gloves, being pulled stiff by the negative box pressure, as if the hands of an invisible man were inside them, the guy asked Craig, "What did the glove box say to the glove?"

Craig had looked perplexed. "I don't know. What?"

"Is that pressure differential, or are you just happy to see me?"

Craig never forgot the joke, and though he had frowned with disapproval at the time, he was now smiling at recalling it.

Fortunately, Dr. Oddlove thought Craig's smile was the result of NA-1's remark about keeping the gas off the plants. If Dr. Oddlove had thought Craig was taking the matter lightly, the consequences would have been serious.

I sensed the near miss and was grateful another crisis had been averted. But I was overwhelmed with concern about Craig's inability to focus his consciousness.

"That's great news, because gas purification is working as designed. The gloves are now hanging limp in the room."

"Good to hear," NA-1 said. "I know you don't know the answer to this yet, Craig, but I'm going to ask it anyway."

"Go ahead, sir."

"What do you think caused the over-pressurization? Was it operator error, a breach in a weld, or maybe a software glitch? What is your best guess?"

Craig had a prepared, canned speech ready. He looked over at Hidebound, who sat ramrod straight in his chair, his eyes boring into Craig.

"I don't really have a guess, sir," Craig said. "You know this facility well, sir, as does Dr. Oddlove. You have already laid out the possibilities; honestly, it could be any of them."

Craig was fully aware that DC had been briefed about the AI issue. NA-1 would have never added software glitch in his list if he hadn't been.

"Which one? That's the question," Craig continued. "There was some confusion in the control room during the loading process. That makes me wonder, but it's too early to speculate. The confusion could have been anything. We will find out."

"Okay, Craig," NA-1 replied. "I expect a briefing tomorrow as well. I want to stay informed. The deputy secretary has been brought up to speed and will cover the incident in his briefing to the secretary tomorrow morning. If you learn anything else meaningful, one of you guys call me so that I can add it to the secretary's briefing."

"Yes, sir," Dr. Oddlove replied. "You will be the first to know. Thank you, sir. Is there anything else?"

"No, that'll do for now. Just keep the gas in the facility and don't miss a shipment," he said.

"Will do, sir."

They exchanged pleasantries, and Stacy and Craig walked out together.

"How do you think it went?" Stacy asked him.

"About as well as it could. No one seemed overly alarmed or, worse, angry. We will just be under constant pressure to fix it."

"Absolutely right about that," Stacy said.

Craig and Stacy split up as she went back to the control room and Craig went to his office. As he entered, Claire asked, "Well, how did it go?"

"Fine. No one was overly concerned, but the facility rep is holding on to this AI glitch thing. I sure hope he's wrong."

"Me too," Claire replied with a sincere smile.

Uh-oh. Craig is vulnerable right now, and Claire is making goo-goo eyes at him. Warning! Warning! Craig's mind was going into the gutter, and I needed to react. I immediately put thoughts of baseball into Craig's consciousness. It was the seventh inning in the regional playoffs in high school. Craig was playing third, and his team was up by one run. The opposing team had a man on first with two outs. The batter hit a single into center field. The runner from first made the mistake of trying for third. The center fielder on Craig's team had a cannon. The throw was over Craig's head, but he made an incredible leap, caught it, and in one sweeping motion tagged the runner out. The crowd went wild. Regional champs! You did it, Craig. This memory always worked. Nothing shut down his libido like baseball.

Craig said, "Thanks, Claire," and sat down at his desk, continuing to relive his glory days of baseball.

Whew! Nicely done. Hey, Jesus, did you see that?

PERSPECTIVE
Fall Leaves (2012)

Craig and Betty finished their Danishes and coffee, and Katy stood to leave.

"I hope that Danish doesn't spoil your breakfast. I need to get to my office; I have a big day ahead."

Craig looked up with love in his eyes and said, "Sure, sweetheart; you go to work."

She hugged Craig. "I love you, Dad."

"I love you too."

Betty was focused on the empty napkin in her lap. She felt nothing except confusion. Katy then leaned over and hugged Betty, who gave a stiff, noncommittal hug back and smiled.

"I'll see you both real soon," Katy said as she headed out the door. She felt confused, but at peace. *I can't believe I'm okay with this*, she thought. *Heck, I can't believe I'm okay lying to my dad nearly every day. And I can't believe I'm getting used to the smell of urine. Who am I?*

As she left Craig's room, she smiled and waved at Thomas, who was wheeling a resident to breakfast. As she punched in her code to exit the Emerald floor, Katy began to pray. *Jesus*, she began, *I hope I'm in your will here. I don't really know what to do or what is right. I need your help today. Please give me strength, but even more than that, give Dad peace. I thank you for the peace I saw in his eyes as I left. Thank you, Lord.*

Thomas was feeling thankful for the opportunity to help the residents of Fall Leaves and their families. His job often brought him a rewarding sense of accomplishment and satisfaction. As he approached the dining area, he saw another one of his favorite residents, Miss Sue, already seated at a table. She was holding a baby doll that was bare except for a diaper. She was caressing the baby and speaking softly to it as she rocked back and forth. The baby was Miss Sue's constant companion. Thomas wasn't sure whether she thought it was a real baby or not, but he knew it kept her calm.

"How is the baby this morning, Miss Sue?"

She didn't acknowledge him; she just kept gently rocking and caressing the doll. Thomas had known Miss Sue for over a year. When she first arrived, she was lost and despondent, prompting her daughter to conduct a little research. Her daughter had read online that a doll, stuffed animal, or pet could help a memory patient overcome depression, so she bought her mom the doll. It pleased Thomas to see how well it was working.

Thomas made a point of getting to know the residents' relatives—the daughters, sons, husbands, and wives of people who so often seemed to Thomas as though they were only shadows of their former selves. He watched as they attended to their loved ones, and he could usually tell a great deal about them by how they expressed their care. When they first arrived at Fall Leaves for a visit, most seemed lost, sad, and confused. Too often, well-meaning family members asked their loved ones a lot of questions, which was generally not a good idea. The residents usually weren't capable of responding, which created stress on both sides. Having meaningful conversations with their loved ones was challenging, which inevitably led to frustration. Thomas saw it on their faces and offered advice when he could. He suggested beginning interactions on a happy note.

Katy had learned this approach from Thomas and was always bright and cheerful when she first saw Craig. A few times she'd simply come in and say hello. That tended to confuse Craig. Another time, she just sat at the table and smiled. Craig had given her a puzzled look and asked her who she was. Although his response devastated her, Katy learned from it. Even so, if she began with a cheerful greeting and a declaration of who she was, Craig would frequently become forgetful if she stayed too long. One time she had taken Craig outside and was sitting in a swing with him. She was truly enjoying the moment, a time of stillness and reflection without worrying about work, emails, or other distractions. Craig seemed at peace that day, but several times while looking at her face, he asked, "Are you my sister?"

Katy learned to deal with it, as she knew Craig didn't see himself as old. She'd just say, "No, Dad. I'm Katy, your daughter." Craig would look puzzled and say, "Oh." If she stayed, he might ask her the same question a few minutes later. Katy knew that his long-term memory was fading and his near-term was nearly gone. He could forget he had eaten breakfast while on his way back to his room from the dining area.

Thomas helped so many of the residents' relatives, but some situations arose that were heartbreaking to him. His worst resident problem was another case of what the other caregivers called a "hookup." It involved Martha, a sixty-eight-year-old woman who had good physical function but was a mess mentally. She became involved with Mike, a resident Thomas disliked. Thomas knew that Mike was confused, but whatever was guiding Mike was evil. Mike took advantage of Martha's confusion and spent a good bit of time with her. He convinced her to go to bed with him numerous times. Thomas discovered the situation and followed the same procedure for Mike and Martha that he had with Craig and Betty. The email from Vanessa was sent to Martha's husband Tony, who was haunted by having to place his beloved wife in a facility. He adored Martha and it pained him greatly to see her at Fall Leaves. He visited her four or five times a week and often sat with her during meals. The news had been more than Tony could take. He was a strong man, self-made and wealthy, but this was something he couldn't handle.

Tony initially blamed Fall Leaves and read Vanessa the riot act. He was furious. However, after his initial outburst, Tony knew he had to resign himself to the truth. Fall Leaves had not caused this; dementia was to blame. He tried hard to accept it, but it was impossible. After the revelation, Thomas remembered seeing Tony sitting with Martha on a sofa in one of the sitting rooms, discussing what had occurred. Tony was tough and wasn't crying, but his face clearly wore the stress and despair he felt as he tried in vain to logically discuss the matter with Martha. As Tony talked, Martha fidgeted with a bag of clothes she had next to her. Finally, Tony grabbed the bag and pulled it away from her. "Are you even listening to me?" he cried out, the anguish in his voice reverberating throughout the room and into the hall where Thomas stood.

It was such an unfortunate situation, one that greatly troubled Thomas. Whenever Tony came to sit with Martha at meals, Mike would sit at a nearby table, staring at them both with a cold smirk. Tony would glare back at Mike as if to say, "I'd like to punch your lights out." Mike's smug demeanor never changed. It was one of the most painful things Thomas had ever witnessed. He believed it would only be a matter of weeks now before Tony moved Martha to another facility, which Thomas believed to be for the best.

As Thomas helped a resident move from the wheelchair to the table, he caught a glimpse of Betty and Craig coming down the hall. They took seats at their usual table beside Olga, who was staring at *The Wall Street Journal*.

"Good morning, Miss Betty and Mr. Craig," Thomas said as he walked to the table. "You both look nice this morning."

Both just regarded him and smiled. Behind Thomas, a man in his early forties was quickly approaching the group. It was Levi, Betty's son. Craig had no idea who Levi was, but he was troubled by his appearance. He simply watched him with a puzzled expression.

I too had an uneasy feeling and was flooded with concern about what might happen next.

"Hey, Levi. Good to see you this morning," Thomas said awkwardly.

Thomas didn't have the same relationship with Levi that he had with Katy, and he was as worried as I was.

Levi was a towering young man, nearly six-foot-seven and weighing a lean 240. He had played tight end for Montana State, where he'd finished second in his class. He wore a loose-fitting T-shirt and jeans. Whenever he arrived, virtually everyone took notice. Normally he was a gentle giant, but today was different. Today he was angry—he had received the email from Vanessa.

"Hello," he replied curtly as he grabbed a seat beside his mom. "Hi, Mom. How did you sleep?" he asked sarcastically.

"Hi there, Levi," Betty answered sweetly. "I'm so glad to see you this morning."

Betty's brain was firing properly; she remembered Levi and felt happy, even though she didn't know why he'd come or why he looked angry. Craig began to feel a bit more trepidation, but he somehow knew to keep quiet.

I was glad. While Craig didn't exactly grasp what was happening, his software easily picked up the potential danger and shut him down.

Thomas went back to the counter and helped Shana deliver the breakfast plates. Olga had already begun picking at her food while intently studying the words of the paper. She momentarily glanced up when Levi spoke but then quickly returned to her reading. As Thomas sat the plates in front of Craig and Betty, he felt the tension in the air. It was thick. It was suffocating. Levi alternated between disapproving glances at his mom and disdainful glares at Craig. Thomas knew he needed to do something. "Could I speak with you for a moment, Levi?"

Levi looked perturbed, hesitated for a few long seconds, and then reluctantly agreed.

"How about we sit and talk for a few minutes while your mom eats her breakfast?" Thomas said, and he led Levi to the adjoining sitting room.

"I guess you know why I'm here."

"I sure do," Thomas replied. "I'd like to answer any questions you have and help in any way I can."

Levi erupted. "What the f—k is going on in this cuckoo's nest? Some creep is now sleeping with my mom? What kind of place is this? I'd like to punch that guy."

Thomas was taken aback by the outburst, but years of practice enabled him to remain calm.

"I truly understand how you feel—"

"Do you?" Levi blurted.

"Yes, I think I do," Thomas said calmly. "Can I start by telling you what happened?"

Levi responded with a sullen shrug, prompting Thomas to cautiously recount the events he had witnessed. He revealed some information about Craig that he knew he shouldn't due to HIPAA restraints, but he did it anyway. It was needed for this situation. Thomas described what he saw and stressed that he had not seen any evidence of coercion or abuse.

Levi reacted, "There is no way you can know that! No way. My mom would never have an affair."

"Are you sure of that?" Thomas countered, feeling the need to push back gently. "They are both very confused. I know them pretty well, especially Mr. Craig. He is a good man but ravaged by his disease. They are both just acting on impulses. Now, I'm not saying I like it either, but Fall Leaves can't encourage or discourage it unless there is evidence of coercion or abuse. I know that seems like a cop-out to you, but it's the truth. However, I would be more than happy to help you in any way I can, Levi. I honestly want what's best for your mom. I mean it."

Levi sighed heavily, not knowing what to say. Thomas made valid points and seemed to be a genuine, caring fellow who wanted to help. After a long pause, Levi looked at Thomas as he successfully fought back a tear forming in his eye.

"I understand the situation, Thomas. I do. But that doesn't help at all. This is my mom, for crying out loud. It's bad enough that my schmuck of a father left her for a trophy wife, but now she's got this creepy old man sleeping with her? It's just not right."

"I know it's not," Thomas replied. "It's part of the dementia. People here often revert back to instinct, and that instinct is not fettered with all the filters and moral lessons they've learned. Somehow those vanish. I have no idea why; I just know that what your mom is doing is not her old self. It's just her instincts. I feel for you, Levi, and it pains me as well."

Levi sensed how sincere Thomas was and finally unclenched his jaw. "Jesus," he said, "What a mess. Look, I'm sorry for what I said earlier. I guess I was feeling unfiltered as well. Maybe it's the company I'm keeping here."

Thomas smiled and said, "Yeah, it's goin' around."

Levi stood up and returned to the table where his mother sat with Craig and Olga. They were still eating slowly, picking at their food with no conversation between them. Levi sat down again, this time with a gentle smile, and said, "Hi, Mom. You look so pretty this morning." Betty's brain again fired correctly.

"Oh, it's Levi, my favorite son. Hi, Levi."

She had no recollection of their meeting not more than ten minutes prior. Levi smiled at his mother and asked if she was enjoying her breakfast. Betty looked perplexed, then nodded her head a few seconds later. Craig watched all of this with no real understanding of what was happening, but his feeling of fear returned. It wasn't paralyzing, but it was real. He somehow knew to keep quiet and avoid any prolonged eye contact.

I was so relieved that Craig kept his mouth shut. Levi clearly didn't approve of Craig's relationship with his mother, and that's a gross understatement.

In the awkward silence all visitors felt, Levi watched the three of them eat their breakfast. It was virtually impossible to carry on any type of conversation without stirring up strange feelings that stressed the residents. Or the comments simply died, fading into a deeper silence that the visitors felt compelled to fill. It was mentally exhausting. Levi, like Katy, knew from experience how futile any attempt at dialogue was, so he chose to sit quietly. Instead of immediately pulling out his phone to escape reality, Levi took a few minutes to reset his view of how his mother was progressing. He did so with heightened awareness of Craig and where she was in the timeline of regression.

I watched helplessly. I was used to that. Then I tried to escape reality and started thinking back to our childhood.

MEMORIES
Cleveland (1954)

C raig grew up near Cleveland with two amazing parents, Al and Alice. He was close to them both, but especially his dad, who had been an engineer for the Cleveland Electric Company. His office was downtown at 55 Public Square, and he often took Craig to work with him. Some of those trips downtown ended with a Tribe evening game.

Craig and I loved those times. We also went to a few Browns games, but Al was more reluctant to take us to those because the atmosphere was much different. Once, the hammered guy sitting next to us started taunting two guys behind him who were donning Steelers coats. The language was unbelievable, and I can still remember Craig's eyes growing as big as saucers. Finally, one of the Steelers fans, who was also drunk, slapped the guy in the back of his head. It was on. The guy next to us dived back and grabbed the Steelers fan's coat, pulling him down. He wedged the guy between his seat and the one in front and commenced a ground and pound on his head. That lasted only a few seconds before the second Steelers fan jumped on the back of the Browns fan.

Al had immediately thrown his body on top of his son to assure he didn't get hurt, while Craig tried to peek under his dad's armpit to see what was happening. Excitement like that didn't just happen every day. It was a major memory, and Craig knew it. However, the whole thing was short-lived as six security guys descended on the melee. They grabbed the brawlers by their coats, dragged them into the aisle, then sat on them. Man, what a day that was! We never forgot it, but neither did Al; we didn't see another Browns game until Craig was fourteen.

As a whole, Craig's childhood was good. Both Al and Alice were devout Christians, though their backgrounds in their faith were much different. Al was raised in a Pentecostal church, whereas Alice was raised in a Methodist church. They both loved God, but the form of worship they were used to was much different. They eventually came to grips with that fact and chose a Baptist church to attend together.

Throughout his life, Al became confused and, at times, disillusioned with formal religion and Christian denominations in general. He read the Bible every day and made a concerted effort to be versed in what he believed and why he believed it. He loved to debate the scriptures and the deeper aspects of his faith. However, Al had learned the hard way that most Christians didn't want to go very deep. Once, he had been discussing the ever popular, yet never resolved, issue of predestination with another member of his church. That discussion ended badly, with the member calling Al an evil heretic.

Al found predestination to be ridiculous. There was no way that God caused all the evil on Earth. How could God predestine that people would molest children or exterminate them in prison camps? There were only two choices. One he called the Milestone Theory and the other the Headbanger Theory. Al's beliefs were best summed up in the Milestone Theory—that God had set the world in motion for His own pleasure, choosing not to know all the events that would occur but keeping His eye on things. This made certain the human experience could only get so bad. God truly wanted His creation to have free will; without it, He was merely forming and assisting robots. However, certain events, like the second coming of Christ, were in fact predestined. These were what Al called Milestones, and he was firmly convinced that the scriptures bore this out. It was clear that God had predestined and orchestrated specific incidents, but others just happened, with God choosing to intervene however and whenever he wanted.

Al's backup theory, the Headbanger Theory, revolved around a simple premise: no one could figure it out because God didn't want us to know, so trying to understand the whole concept was like banging your head against a wall. Al was comfortable with this assumption, though he preferred the Milestone Theory. He acknowledged that he viewed the whole thing through a cloudy glass, never insinuating he had all the answers. However, the straightforward predestination theory drove him nuts.

Al also believed that Christian denominations were divisive. He had heard Baptist ministers preach that Pentecostals were in a cult and that their form of worship was satanic. He had been in Pentecostal services where preachers claimed that Catholics were eternally doomed for praying to Mary and relying on their "evil" symbols. Al despised it all. He believed that the denominations should just be forms of worship; that some folks needed a more formal and sterile worship, like the Methodists or Catholics, whereas others let it all out, like the Pentecostals. What really mattered to Al was a belief in Christ as the son of God, forgiveness of sin through Him, and the working out of one's own salvation with fear and trembling. Beyond that, it was up to the individual to decide, and God would be the ultimate judge, no one else.

Possibly as a result of his parents' faith, Craig, at the age of eight, accepted Christ. It happened in his Sunday school class at

Bay Village Grace Baptist, a church his family attended together. Craig's teacher, Mrs. Fowler, had just explained John 3:16, which said, "For God so loved the world that he gave his only begotten son, that whosoever shall believe in him shall not perish, but have eternal life."

As Mrs. Fowler spoke, Craig and I felt a strange feeling, like we needed something and deeply longed for it. Craig raised his hand and asked Mrs. Fowler what the verse meant. Mrs. Fowler then explained the plan of salvation to the class. Christ had died for our sins, she said, and if we ask him to forgive our sins, believe in him as God's son, and turn our lives over to him, we are born again. Craig was mesmerized and knew he wanted in. I was convinced too. I'd like to take credit for it, but Craig's software actually seemed to want it too. Something miraculous happened that morning. I still don't fully understand it, but those ten minutes in that class changed our life forever.

As we got in the car after the morning worship service, Al asked if anyone wanted to go out for brunch. Craig heartily agreed, then proceeded to tell his parents what had happened in class. They reacted to his news as if they had just won the lottery. I still remember the joyous look on their faces. There has never been a better moment in my life. Al pulled the car over in front of the Avon Lake coal-fired generating facility— and from that day forward I always had a fond spot for that place—and turned around to look Craig in the eyes. Al had a tear streaming down his cheek. It was the first time we had seen him cry.

"This is the best news I've ever had," Al said. We were a bit surprised by all the fuss, but it felt good. We felt clean and new and felt a closer bond to our parents. This was even better than before, and it just kept getting better.

That Sunday morning lives in me and Craig as the biggest day of our life, even though I'm still not exactly sure what *happened. I mean, I know I became a Christian and began to work out how to integrate my new faith into what I did and how I controlled Craig, but what really happened there? I knew I heard a voice. It wasn't a literal voice, but a voice nonetheless. Or maybe I should call it more of a supernatural pull. Whatever it was, that voice or pull was definitely real. But where did it come from, and how did it find me? I can always tell when I'm battling Craig's software, struggling against the desire to do stuff we shouldn't, but this was different. It wasn't Craig. I'm sure this was God talking to us. He was actually drawing Craig and me toward His plan of salvation.*

That day in the car in front of the Avon Lake smoke belcher changed the whole family; it was as if they all had a new common purpose. Al began to talk differently about right and wrong to Craig. He seemed to become much more careful about what he said, giving God more credit. He also began saying he would pray, not just think, about things.

The family continued attending Bay Village Grace Baptist, but Al became less enthralled with that church. Though he seldom openly criticized the church or pastor, it became clear that Al's compromise with Alice on this was just that, a compromise. He was feeling stifled. One Sunday evening, Al announced that he was going to attend the Avon Church of God. He didn't tell anyone until about an hour before he planned to leave.

I think Al felt like he needed a dose of Pentecost or something. My guess is that he just had a longing for his past. Anyway, he looked at Craig and asked if he wanted to go too. Craig was shocked and bummed out. He had just finished studying for a test the next day and wanted to watch TV. I wanted to go and wanted to go badly. I immediately went to work on Craig and made him feel guilty. I told him that Jesus would be disappointed if we didn't go, and we didn't want that. Craig paused for a minute, then agreed.

Alice was caught off guard. She had never felt comfortable at a Pentecostal church and didn't know why Craig needed to go. She gave Al a perplexed and somewhat displeased look. "You don't have to go," she told Craig, "but it's up to you." She didn't want Craig to sense her disapproval or the fact that she and Al weren't on the same page.

I jumped back in with both feet, warning Craig of the perils of staying home. Jesus may see to it that he gets an F on his test tomorrow, or worse. Craig, thoroughly confused, paused again before finally agreeing to go.

"Come on. We'll stop for a burger on the way home," Al said.

When they arrived at Avon Church of God a few minutes before the seven o'clock service, they sat in a pew on the far side of the church toward the back, the same area that Al and his family had sat when he was a kid.

The church itself looked like most Churches of God. (Whoever is in charge of these churches must get a deal on building materials and follow the same design plan.) Church members entered the long A-frame structure through the foyer with several offices branching off of it, then went through two wooden doors that were opened and held to the wall with door stops. Rows of wooden pews filled the sanctuary with a center aisle and one running down each side. The center aisle led to a platform that covered the entire front of the church. Three stairs that spanned the length of the platform led to a wooden pulpit. It was nicely stained, but in no way ornate. About five feet behind the pulpit were four wooden chairs, two on each side. At the back of the stage, a wooden covering on the floor could be removed to reveal a baptism pool beneath it. Changing rooms to prepare for and exit from the dunkings were on either side of the pool. Elevated above it was a wooden cross, illuminated by spotlights. On one side of the platform was an upright piano; an organ was positioned on the other side. The windows were frosted glass.

The church looked like it might hold two hundred or so people, but there were no more than thirty there when Craig and Al arrived. No one sat within three pews of them. Craig had no idea about what might happen. All he was thinking about was the TV he was missing. As he scanned the congregation, he caught a glimpse of a young girl on the other side of the church. She was really pretty. She had long hair and was wearing a dress. *Maybe this will be better than I anticipated*, Craig thought. The young girl was sitting with a woman who looked to be her mother. She had a dress on and donned one of those old-fashioned buns, with all her hair pulled up on top of her head in a giant lump. In fact, Craig noticed that all the women wore dresses and looked a bit plain. None wore makeup or jewelry.

The pianist was playing a song Craig had never heard, but it soothed us both. Just then, a big guy wearing what looked like an old pair of dress slacks and a fairly wrinkled button-down shirt tapped Al on the shoulder.

"Hello," said the man. "Welcome. This your first time here?"

"Yes, it is," Al responded with a smile. "We thought we'd come and worship with you tonight. This is my son Craig." Craig looked up and nodded his head.

I would later come to understand the important message Al was sending when he said "come to worship," which was code for "we're Christians and there's no need to come and get us if we don't go up front during the altar call."

The man said, "Oh, wonderful! Well again, welcome." He then left and went to the back of the church.

At seven o'clock, a large man made his way onto the platform and sat in one of the chairs behind the pulpit. He was wearing a black suit and tie and was holding a black Bible. His graying, black hair was slicked back, giving him a serious appearance. He looked like an overweight Johnny Cash.

A young woman stood in front of the pulpit and spoke loudly. "Please rise," she instructed. "Let's begin by singing 'Meeting in the Air' together." The pianist began to play as she started to sing.

Craig stood with Al. He'd never heard the song before and listened intently as Al sang along, apparently having learned it when he was younger. Occasionally, though, Craig snuck glances at the young girl across the way. She felt Craig's gazes but didn't look over.

When the song was finished, the lady on the platform told the crowd to be seated, and the man in the dark suit stepped to the pulpit. "Praise God," he started. "It's good to be in the house of the Lord tonight." Craig surveyed the sanctuary. Most of the pews were empty or had just a few people in them. Craig wondered where everyone was. Maybe they were home watching TV. That's where he wished he was; that is, unless the girl across the aisle came over and sat by him.

The man at the pulpit had moved on to prayer requests. "We have much to pray about tonight. First, let's pray for those who couldn't be with us tonight." He smiled in a stern sort of way and went on. "Please pray for Sister Christa; she is home with her back again. She needs a miracle healing. Also, please pray for Brother Bill who is still battling the cancer in his prostate. He has an appointment tomorrow to decide what he will do as far as treatment goes. I know I will be fasting and praying tomorrow for him. If you feel led, please join me."

The man speaking was Pastor Kinsman. He had been the pastor there for over twenty years and ran the church as if it were totally his own. Being the pastor of a Pentecostal church required a strong leader. First, there were the rules to enforce, things like no swimming with the opposite sex, no movies, no pants or short hair for women, no smoking, no drinking, and on and on. Then there was the management of the services that could quickly get out of hand, once the Spirit moved, if people participating didn't control themselves.

Al knew all of this from the time he had spent attending Pentecostal churches as a child. However, as part of his journey to his own salvation, he came to believe that while the people who had made up these rules had the best of intentions, they were just interpretations of what men thought God meant by not being worldly. Al didn't personally believe in them, but if the people in these congregations felt they needed to obey them, it was fine with him. Al went to church that night for that feeling he missed when he could openly praise God and feel the presence of the Holy Spirit in the sanctuary. It was a feeling of incredible and indescribable peace. It was as if his inner being had been washed clean again, and all his concerns diminished to trivia. He loved that feeling but didn't choose to attend a church that was so staunch in its rule enforcement.

Pastor Kinsman finished with his list of prayer requests and led the congregation in prayer. He had a deep and almost scary tone to his voice, and it was clear that he meant business. Craig looked over at the girl across the aisle again. Her eyes were open, and she wasn't really praying. She suddenly turned her head and saw that Craig was looking at her. She gave him a quick smile, then turned back toward the platform and closed her eyes.

The pastor then stepped back to his chair and the lady who led the first song came back and asked everyone to open their hymnals. Just then, an older lady with gray hair in the uniform bun stood up and started saying something loudly that made no sense to Craig. She was speaking in tongues. Craig just watched with astonishment. He looked over at his dad, who had his eyes closed. Craig elbowed his dad, who then opened his eyes. "Shhhh," Al said in a manner that wasn't mean or condemning. "I'll explain on our way home." The girl across the aisle had her eyes closed too, so Craig followed suit.

When she finished speaking, total silence blanketed the congregation. Craig could hear his heart beating. After what seemed like a lifetime, the pastor came forward to the microphone. He began to speak as if he were reading, but he wasn't. "I am the Lord, your God," he began. "I work in strange and mysterious ways. I am with you tonight and always. I give and take away. I am with Brother Bill and all those sick among you. I will heal and make whole all that come to me with pure hearts. I am the Lord, your God." The pastor was finished. He waited a few seconds and walked back to his seat.

The lady beside him then led the congregation in several songs. Craig felt the joy in the people's voices. They were truly enjoying the experience. Craig wasn't used to this type of worship. At Bay Village Grace Baptist, things were much more formal.

After the singing, Pastor Kinsman began his sermon. He read from 2 Corinthians Chapter 6: "I will live with them and walk with them, and I will be their God and they will be my people. Therefore, come out from them and be separate, says the Lord." He explained in no uncertain terms what the verse meant to the congregation, saying that separation from the world was what God wanted, and that the church should live by the rules God had given them. He gave a few examples but mostly focused on drinking and smoking.

Craig was a bit confused, but then again, he wasn't really giving the sermon his full attention. He was daydreaming about the girl across the way. Al, however, was sitting stoically and listening carefully. The sermon demonstrated exactly what Al disliked about the Pentecostals. They were judgmental and rules based. Nevertheless, Al had felt God's presence during the service, which confused him. If these people were so far out of line, why would God be there? Maybe they were right.

As the pastor finished his sermon, he asked if anyone in the congregation had not yet invited Jesus into their life. This was an altar call. Throughout the service, Al had raised his hands, a subconscious way for him to let others know that he was already a Christian. After no one responded, Pastor Kinsman closed the service with a final prayer.

As Al and Craig made their way toward the exit, a man in front of them struck up a conversation with Al. "Are you a first-time visitor?" the man asked.

"Yes," Al responded and then went on to tell him that they were already church members who wanted a dose of Sunday night preaching since their church only had morning services.

While the men talked, Craig eyed the pretty girl, who was heading out with her mother. *Come on, Dad*, Craig thought. *Let's go.* He was hoping for at least a "hello" on their way out, but it was too late. She was gone, likely out of his life forever.

Craig and Al made their way to the car. As he cranked the engine, Al asked, "So what did you think?"

"It was fine, Dad, but I've got a few questions."

"Sure. Fire away."

"Well," Craig began, "What was that lady who stood up saying, the one speaking some other language?"

"That was a message in tongues. She felt that God wanted her to convey a message to the congregation."

"Really?" Craig marveled.

"Yes, and the pastor then interpreted what she said."

"No kidding!" Craig said. "Why don't we do that in our church?"

"That's complicated, son. Fully explaining it will take some time, but the short answer is that it's just a form of worship our church doesn't embrace. The form of worship you saw tonight was different, but real. It's not for everyone. That's the beauty of Christianity—there are many ways to seek and worship God. You can do it in a very formal way like the Catholics, or you can be less inhibited like you saw tonight. Neither is necessarily better;

it's just what you are most comfortable with. The thing that is important is that you know Jesus, have him as your savior, and are trying to live for him. What's beyond that is much less important."

"Okay, Dad. Sounds good. We still stopping for a burger?"

"You bet," Al replied.

Al was pleased with his decision to bring Craig to a different church. He went to church that night and took Craig along for two reasons. First, Al missed the move of the Spirit and the peace it brought. It was a part of his past that he truly missed. However, as he grew up, he found it uncomfortable to invite someone to go to church with him. They would be freaked out if someone spoke in tongues or marched around the church waving their hands. He just couldn't bring himself to invite friends for fear that news would spread of it and he would be considered a wacko at school. As a result, Al kept his school friends and church friends separate. It had made him sad, but he felt it was necessary. Second, he wanted Craig to at least be exposed to a Pentecostal service. He would leave the rest up to God. Al honestly believed that the most important thing was that Craig accepted Christ, but for some reason he still wanted Craig to experience it.

When they arrived home, Craig greeted his mom before heading toward the stairs and his room. Alice stood up and said, "Hey, did you guys eat?"

"Yeah. We stopped for fast food. I'm going upstairs. Good night."

"Wait a minute. How did you like the church?"

"It was okay; kinda weird, though. There were only a few people there and Dad had to explain what was going on. I didn't really get it, but it seemed okay, I guess."

Alice gave Al the same look of disapproval she had given him before they left, but this look also had an air of relief to it. She was happy that Craig wasn't freaked out and also happy that he didn't seem to be drawn to it.

Craig walked up the stairs, and Alice followed Al into the family room where he sat down on the sofa. "Why did you feel you needed to go to a Pentecostal church? Why did you take Craig? Aren't you happy with our church?"

Al had anticipated her questions and already thought through his response. "I think life is a smorgasbord and you need to try it all, even if you end up not liking some of it."

Alice looked at Al with a smirk. "Don't give me that line again."

"Why not? I know I use that line a lot, but it fits here. I want Craig to be able to decide for himself how he wants to worship and serve God. I'd like for him to attend a Catholic church too."

"Okay, I guess I can understand that, but why did *you* want to go? Just to take Craig?" This was a loaded question; she knew Al had wanted to go himself.

"To be honest, honey, 'I needed a shot of love' as Dylan would say." Her smirk intensified as he continued. "I missed the move of the Spirit in the way it happens at a Pentecostal church. I can feel God in our church, and I love going there, but I had a hankering for something more. Don't worry, I don't plan to go back regularly; it's just too awkward. The people there are so sincere and want to be close to God. However, the rules and condemnation that you get kills the deal for me. They are well meaning, and they seem to love God, but they're way off track in trying to establish a code of conduct for all Christians. I started the discussion with Craig, but we just scratched the surface. I just want him to know all that."

"Okay," Alice conceded. "I feel better about it now."

This entire experience had been a surprise to me. Looking back, it seems odd that I immediately knew to push Craig toward attending church that night. His software was fighting it, so I needed to jump in. I'm not sure why I wanted us to go. Maybe it was that other pulling force I felt when Craig accepted Christ. Maybe God was telling me to get Craig to go, whatever the reason.

OPPORTUNITIES
Fall Leaves (2012)

Craig and Betty finished breakfast and sat quietly with Olga and Levi.

"We need to leave soon to see the doctor, Mom," Levi said. He'd been checking his emails while she ate, waiting for her to finish. "We need to go to your room now so we can get ready to leave."

"Okay," Betty replied.

Her response made Craig sad and prompted an unaccustomed feeling of emptiness. He wanted to say something to Levi but felt a bit afraid and confused. He kept quiet.

"Let's go, Mom," Levi said as he stood up.

Betty rose as well and followed Levi to her room. Neither Betty nor Levi spoke directly to Craig, who remained seated, staring into space. The despair and hollowness inside him increased.

Levi entered his mother's room and sat down. Betty did the same, smiling at her son. After about a minute of silence, Levi turned to his mom. "So, you're seeing this Craig guy now? Is that right?"

Betty just stared back at him, then she uttered, "Who?"

"Craig, the guy we just left at the breakfast table."

Betty sat quietly for a moment trying to formulate an answer, but she couldn't.

"You know, Mom, you slept with him last night."

"I did?" Betty shook her head. "Oh no, I don't think so. I sleep in this room; it's mine."

"No, Mom, you slept with that creepy guy Craig last night. How could you?"

Tears began welling up in Betty's mournful and questioning eyes. "I did?"

"Yes. You did. How could you? You need to stop seeing him. It's just not right, and the guy is weird."

"Okay. If I did that, then I'll stop." She choked on her words as tears streamed down her face. "Are you mad at me?" she asked with a look that crushed Levi.

"No, Mom. I'm not mad at you. I love you so much and want you to be safe and happy. I just don't understand what you see in that guy."

"What guy?"

Confused, Levi couldn't tell if his mom was being coy or if she really didn't remember, but her tears and shattered expression were more than he could take. He began to cry as well. He stood up and walked the few steps to where his mom was sitting. He knelt, hugged her, and pulled her close, his tears mixing with hers.

"I love you, Mom. You're everything to me."

Levi truly loved Betty, but he felt helpless. His guilt about placing her in the facility was back and more powerful than ever. How could he leave her here knowing that, in all likelihood, she would continue to see Craig?

"We have a doctor's appointment today," he said, wiping his eyes. "It'll take us an hour to get there, so we need to get going soon. I thought that after the appointment we could go out to lunch and maybe get an ice cream."

"Oh, that would be great!" Betty happily exclaimed, having forgotten all about the sadness she had felt only a few minutes earlier. "Should I get dressed up?"

"No. You look fine just as you are, but let's go into the bathroom and comb your hair just a bit," Levi replied.

＊＊

Back in the dining area, Craig was more confused than ever. After a few rocks in his chair, he was able to push off of the floor and make it to his feet. Out of instinct, he pushed his chair back and began heading down the hall. Again, the tinge of sorrow pricked him as he walked slowly to his room. He opened his door, sat on the love seat, picked up the remote, and turned on the TV. His eyes were glued to the screen, although he was totally unaware of what he was watching. After a few minutes, he heard a knock on his door.

"It's me, Mr. Craig," Thomas said as he came in. Craig looked up sadly and said nothing.

"You okay?"

Craig pondered Thomas for a moment and then said, "What do you want?"

"Just want to make sure you're okay, Mr. Craig. You're going to exercise class in a few minutes. Wanted to make sure you were ready."

"I don't need to exercise," Craig said.

"Yes, you do. You are the best athlete in the facility, and all the girls will be sad if their stud isn't there."

Thomas expected a smile and a change of heart. He wasn't disappointed.

"Well, I guess I should go then."

"Right," said Thomas. "Let's go. We can do some warm-ups before the others get there."

In her office, Katy was working on her most important case, reading discovery responses to requests she'd served in a wrongful death suit filed against UPS. Her client's husband was killed after a UPS driver ran a red light and broadsided his car. He died a few days after the crash. Katy stood to make thirty-five percent of a potential monster settlement for her firm; needless to say, she briefed her managing partner weekly on her progress. The case centered around proving that the culture at UPS drove drivers to do whatever was necessary to stay on schedule. She strove to show that UPS was intentionally, or at least negligently, responsible for the dangerous behavior of the driver. The case was a career maker. Even so, Katy was having trouble focusing on the tedious and minimal responses the UPS attorneys had provided, not much more than the company's policies on scheduling and timelines. As she read the documents, Katy's mind wandered to Craig. The picture of him lying in bed with Betty was seared on her mind. Thinking about it for a few moments, she felt compelled to stop by and see him after work, regardless of what she might see when she got there. She then directed her attention back to the UPS scheduling policy.

**

An awkward fog of silence filled Levi's car as he drove his mom to the neurologist for her semiannual evaluation. Betty's absentminded stare remained focused on the road ahead. Levi struggled to find the words to say to her.

"The doctor is going to be asking you some questions, Mom, so when we get there just be ready to talk to him, okay?"

Betty turned to her son. "What kind of questions?"

"Just some questions about you and what you've been up to."

"Why?" Betty asked. Levi paused as he had once again painted himself into a corner. He couldn't tell her the truth for fear she'd cry, and while he didn't want to lie, he felt he had no choice.

"It's just part of everyone's physical as they get older, Mom. I'll be doing the same thing soon too. Just normal stuff to make sure you're still fit."

"Oh. Okay then."

They sat in the neurologist's office waiting room until the nurse called for Betty. They followed the nurse to the exam room where they waited again. After a few minutes, a young woman came in and introduced herself as Laura. "I'm Dr. Pons's physician's assistant, and I will be performing the assessment today for Dr. Pons to review," she explained.

After a few minutes of small talk, the PA sat down and opened her laptop. "I'm going to ask you some questions, Betty. Is that okay?"

Betty looked puzzled and a bit nervous, but in a shy and tepid voice, she agreed. The PA plowed through a litany of questions about current events, dates, and past experiences that had been added to her questionnaire from prior meetings. The whole thing was over in about twenty minutes.

"That's it," Laura said, smiling kindly. "You and your son can go back out front now. Dr. Pons will meet with you just as soon as he's able to go over the results." She then led Levi and Betty back to the waiting room.

After what seemed like days, but was actually about half an hour, Levi was called back.

"I'm going back to see the doctor," Levi told his mom. He was a bit leery of leaving Betty alone, so he asked the attendant at the front desk to watch his mom while he met with Dr. Pons.

"Sure," she said. "It's part of my job. She'll be just fine, and if I need you, I'll come and get you."

Levi took a seat in one of the two leather chairs in front of the doctor's large and ornate wooden desk. Dr. Pons was seated behind the desk in a leather swivel chair reviewing Betty's results on his desktop. Behind him, surrounded by framed diplomas and various official-looking certificates, was a painting of a man seated on a rock by the sea. The man was peacefully looking out at the water as if waiting for someone to return.

"Hello, Levi," the doctor said, giving a quick and professional smile before returning to his computer. "How's your mom doing?"

Levi hesitated for a minute. "Not so great."

Dr. Pons met his eyes and asked, "Oh really? Why?"

"Well, I received information this week that Mom is involved with another patient at her facility."

"Involved?" the doctor asked.

"Yes, apparently the staff found Mom in bed with a man who lives there too. The word is, she wasn't coerced—Mom did so willingly—but I'm having a hard time believing that."

"I see," Dr. Pons replied in a monotone voice. "Let me address that as part of the assessment I want to give you. Is that okay?"

"I guess so," Levi replied, feeling a bit put off by the doctor's refusal to directly address the issue.

"Your mom's Alzheimer's disease has progressed a bit over the past six months," the doctor began, "but she is still functioning pretty well. Her responses are about the same, but I do see some additional confusion about her past, which tells me the disease is advancing. I can't tell you how rapidly it will happen; we'll just have to see. She is already on several medications that can slow the progress, but as we've discussed, there is no cure at this time."

Dr. Pons paused and cleared his throat, then leaned forward in his chair, resting his elbows on the desk. "Regarding her relationship with the man at her facility, I can imagine how it must make you feel. However, it is quite common, though not generally pleasant for the family."

"Boy, do I know it," Levi responded, suddenly feeling his stomach twist.

"I totally understand your feelings," Dr. Pons continued. "The burden of deciding what is the best course of action rests on you and your family. I won't sugarcoat it; it has to be your call. What I usually tell my patients' families is that they should do what they feel is right for the patient, not them. That may sound cold, but I believe it is sound advice. While it may be horrifying for you to think that your mom is in bed with a stranger, it might actually be best for her. Given my limited knowledge of what is happening, I honestly don't have the answer, so I am in no way advising you to let it continue. However, to be honest, without moving her from the facility, there is likely little you will be able to do to stop it. She won't remember that you told her to stop, and the facility's hands are tied in trying to help you stop it."

Well, isn't he a champion of the obvious? Levi thought as he listened to the doctor. *This guy is as cover-your-ass as the facility.*

"So, it's all on me?" Levi asked.

"Yes, it is. This disease takes no prisoners. Everyone gets hurt. I wish it weren't so, but the family gets hurt the worse. I'm sorry."

Levi knew the doctor was right, but that didn't make his life any easier.

Dr. Pons added, "Levi, remember that moving your mom will likely adversely affect her. The more stable she is, the better. I don't say that to attempt to dissuade you from moving her, just to give you information for your decision."

"Okay, Doc," Levi said as he rose to his feet. "I'll take it into consideration. I think I may leave her there for now and watch as things progress, but I'm not sure."

"Feel free to call at any time if you have questions," the doctor told him.

Levi walked to the waiting room and found Betty still seated where he'd left her. She looked up at him without a word. "Let's go, Mom. Let's go to lunch."

Betty stood up on command and followed Levi out the door. He decided to hang out with his mom all day. He knew it would be taxing, but he felt compelled. He had taken the day off anyway, and perhaps he could reason with her about the affair. However, as they walked into the elevator to take them to the parking garage, he doubted it.

Levi and Betty walked to his new SUV, a white Chevy Tahoe with tan leather seats. He opened the door for Betty.

"This is a nice car, Levi," she told him again. Levi knew it wasn't easy for her to get into the vehicle, so he took her arm as she stepped onto the running board. She froze, exactly as she did in the Fall Leaves parking lot; she had no idea how to negotiate her way into the seat.

"Grab onto the handle here," Levi instructed her. She did as he commanded but still had no idea what to do next. "Pull yourself up, and then swing into the seat."

She attempted to do what he said but couldn't pull herself up, which took him by surprise. His mother had always been in good physical shape and still looked to be. However, her dementia limited her peripheral vision and made her much less functional. She hadn't had this much trouble when they left Fall Leaves, but now she was helpless.

Levi put his big right hand softly on Betty's upper thigh and helped hoist her up. She made it and swiveled into the seat. He momentarily felt guilty when he remembered that she didn't have as much difficulty getting into his Camry, and he blamed himself for trading it in for the SUV, which he loved due to his height. Deep down, he knew it wasn't his fault. He closed the door, went around the vehicle, and got into the driver's seat. He backed out and began their journey to the Mexican restaurant he was taking her to for lunch. It had been a family favorite over the years since Betty loved Mexican food. He wondered if she still did.

They arrived, and Levi helped get Betty out and into the restaurant. So far, the whole trip had been much more difficult and mentally taxing than he'd imagined.

Betty stared at the menu as the waitress brought salsa and chips. "Have you decided what you'll have?" she asked.

Betty looked puzzled and a little afraid as she looked up from the menu. Levi was uncertain if he should order for her or let her do it. As Betty looked at the waitress, the awkward pause continued.

"I'll order for us both, ma'am. I'll have the chicken taco plate, and my mother will have the burrito supreme."

The waitress thanked them, took their menus, and returned to the kitchen, leaving Levi and Betty in an uncomfortable silence. Visions of his mother in bed with the creepy guy raced through Levi's consciousness. *What to do?* he asked himself. *What to do?*

He knew questioning his mother was fruitless, but he felt he had to. "Do you like your apartment, Mom?" he asked.

"What apartment?"

"The one where you live."

"Oh. Sure," she said. "I think I like it just fine."

"Do you have a new friend there?" Levi asked.

"I don't know. Do I?"

"Yes, you do, Mom. I think his name is Craig. Do you like him?"

"I guess I do, but I'm not exactly sure."

"Well, Mom, you do have a new friend named Craig, and apparently you are sleeping with him."

Betty's mind suddenly began to fire. "No! I would never sleep with another man besides your father. I love him too much."

Levi was totally frustrated as he paused to ponder her response. He then tried to brush it off and end the conversation, being reminded once again that initiating logical discussions requiring short-term memory was futile.

"Of course you wouldn't," he said, grabbing her hand and giving it a little squeeze. "I was just kidding."

For the remainder of the day, he would simply talk about the here and now and keep it light and positive. There was no other choice.

***

Shortly before five o'clock, Katy was en route from her office to visit her dad. She left work early with the hope of joining him for dinner and assessing his new relationship further. As she arrived in the parking lot of Fall Leaves, Levi was also pulling in with Betty. Katy saw the two of them and was immediately stressed at the thought of walking in with her dad's new girlfriend and son.

Katy exited her car as Levi was helping Betty out of his SUV. She watched as Levi talked her through stepping onto the running board while swiveling and using the handle. He ended up having to steady her thigh as she made it safely to the ground.

"Hey there," Katy said from across the parking lot. Levi looked at Katy and recognized her as Craig's daughter. They only met once or twice and had never really had a meaningful conversation.

"Hey," Levi replied.

Katy waited as Levi and Betty came toward her so she could walk in with them. They moved toward the door as Katy introduced herself. "I'm Katy, and I'm here to visit my dad, Craig. I think we've met before."

"Yes, we have. I'm Levi, and this is my mother, Betty."

"Oh, I know Betty. She eats most meals with my dad." Katy was just talking out of reflex and immediately knew that she was being intentionally coy. She didn't know if Levi was aware of the new relationship, but she suddenly felt like a phony and feared Levi would think she was either stupid or pretending to be naive if he did know about the affair.

They made their way through the lower lobby and headed for the elevator to get to the second floor. The blanket of silent awkwardness in the elevator was overwhelming. Katy broke the silence by saying, "Where have y'all been?"

"I took Mom out for the day," Levi replied emotionlessly. "She had a doctor's appointment, and then we spent the rest of the day together."

Katy was impressed. She knew how challenging it was to be with her dad for more than half an hour. The awkwardness of it was so tiring. She began to see Levi as a loving and protective son.

They exited the elevator, and Katy entered the code to get into the Emerald floor. As they walked in, they could see that the cafeteria area was already populated with residents waiting for dinner. Craig was already seated at his table alone. He looked pitiful. It was as if he had just lost something very valuable to him and had no way to find it.

"Hey, Dad," Katy said in the most enthusiastic voice she could muster, given the very uncomfortable situation. Craig looked up and his brain began to fire. The word "dad" had caused the firestorm.

"Hey, beautiful, young lawyer daughter of mine. How you doing?" As Craig looked at Katy, he saw that Betty was with her. So was that big young man who made him nervous. He was flooded with a barrage of emotions that he couldn't sort out.

Uh-oh. This could be bad. Talk about a potential food fight! An unmitigated disaster. I tried desperately to steer Craig's mind away from Betty, but it was no use. His software was fixated on her, and he was suppressing his fear of Levi. Come on, Craig, I urged. This guy could pinch your head off for shacking up with his mom. Don't come on to Betty now. You could initiate Armageddon. It was useless.

"Who is the pretty lady with you, Katy?" Craig asked.

"This is Betty. You know her; she eats with you every day."

"She does? She sure is pretty."

Levi looked like he had just been eye-gouged by a linebacker. His eyes squinted as he tried to hold his tongue. The fierce glare he directed at Craig signaled his desire to beat him senseless.

Katy immediately felt the anger oozing from Levi and tried to disarm it. "That's sweet, Dad. She sure is pretty. This is her son, Levi."

Suddenly the fear came back to Craig as he looked at the angry young man standing over him. The smile on his face left and the lost gaze returned.

Phew! I was glad.

"Have a seat, Mom," Levi uttered in a perturbed voice. "Sit where you always sit, at least for now."

Katy caught the meaning of Levi's statement. Naturally, he was being protective of his mother, and Katy understood what he wasn't saying. His terse comment suggested that he was aware of the budding relationship between Craig and Betty and was obviously not in favor of it. Katy felt overwhelmed and uncertain about how to handle the delicate situation. She immediately whispered a prayer for help.

As they all sat around the table, Katy looked over at Levi and said, "Can we talk for a few minutes?"

"I guess so."

On their way to the sitting room, they ran into Thomas, who was coming down the hall. He immediately knew what was going on.

"Hey, Katy and Levi, how y'all doing?" Levi said nothing, but Katy felt as if her prayer had been answered.

"Doing well," she replied. "Levi and I were just going to talk for a few minutes. Thomas, could you join us?" Katy silently whispered a prayer of thanks. She felt the conversation with Levi would go better if Thomas was a part of it.

"Sure. Be happy to." Thomas sat in the chair next to Katy while Levi sat on the couch across from them. Katy's mind was whirling with thoughts of how best to start the difficult conversation. She was stressed. Thomas caught it immediately and stepped in.

"Let me start this discussion, if that's okay," Thomas began.

"Sure," said Katy in a relieved voice that was obvious to both Levi and Thomas.

"I know you both have been notified of the recent events between your parents, but I'd like to address your thoughts well beyond what was in the notice."

"Notice," Levi began, laughing briefly with derision. "I got that notice and it was meaningless. How can this facility let something like this happen, much less continue? I'm so pissed off, and I am definitely weighing my options."

"I totally understand your feelings," Thomas said gently. "It's natural."

Katy wanted to speak but was more than happy to let Thomas handle it for now. Normally, she would have joined right in the debate but felt she needed to wait.

Thomas continued, "Having your mother sleep with a stranger would be a devastating event for any good son, and I know you are a good son who loves his mother."

"Don't patronize me," Levi snorted. "You barely know me."

"Of course. I'm sorry if I offended you. It was meant as a compliment."

Katy was amazed at how Thomas was handling the situation without losing his cool. *He'd be an excellent lawyer*, she thought.

"Katy here had, and maybe still has, some of the same feelings you are having. She went through the same range of emotions that you are going through. So, if it's okay, I'd like to give you my thoughts on this," Thomas said.

Levi still looked annoyed and primed to storm off at a moment's notice. However, he sat still, and eventually said, "Go on."

"While it's almost always unpleasant," Thomas began, "this type of situation is common in memory care facilities. The folks here have had major mind changes, and for many that means their inhibitions have been reduced or eliminated. In some cases, they have donned totally new personalities. I'm not a neurologist, but I have plenty of firsthand experience. I know Miss Betty and Mr. Craig very well and love them both. I really do. They are both great souls, but their minds have changed so drastically that it almost seems like there are two different people inside each of them."

Thomas took a deep breath. "I'm not sure how it all works. But let's start with Mr. Craig. He is a nice man who loves his daughter and misses his wife, at least when he's lucid. He is a devout Christian and has led a full and productive life. I see this side of him, but only part of the time." He paused, turning to Katy. "The other part of the time, he is lost. He truly doesn't know where he is or even who he is. It is in those times that he seems to be someone else. I'm in no way saying that *that* Mr. Craig is evil or bad or ill-intentioned. He is just different. He is confused and lost. In those times, it's as if he has forgotten the things in his past that made him who he is or was. It's sad, so I watch for and treasure the real Mr. Craig whenever he comes back."

Katy nodded, feeling a knot in her throat.

"And honestly, Levi, the same is true for your mom," Thomas said. "I know what a great mom she was to you and your brothers and I know how much you love her, just as Katy loves Mr. Craig. However, this disease has changed her. She's still the same Miss Betty sometimes, but not always. I know you can't believe she would get involved with another man, but it happened."

Thomas watched Levi's face, noting the deep line that had appeared between his eyebrows and the muscles in his jaw working tightly. He added, "I know you are angry about this, Levi, and that is natural for a man who cares for his mother's well-being, but perhaps you can begin to look at it in a different way."

Katy began to feel a bit nervous, fearing Thomas had gone too far, potentially setting Levi off in a fit of anger. She whispered another prayer and then said, "I know where Thomas is going with this, and it is awkward for him, given his position at Fall Leaves, so let me chime in for a minute. I too was horrified when I heard of the relationship. I got the same email you did and was so ticked off and confused I could barely think straight. However, I woke up the next morning with a deep feeling of peace. I'm not sure of your faith Levi, but for me, I felt that God had given me that peace."

Levi made eye contact with her. She dared not go into her Bible readings about David for fear it would just enrage him, but she continued, "It was as if I had taken on a whole new mindset. I mean, my dad is lost most of the time now. He just sits and stares, and when he speaks it's often coarse. But as Thomas said, the real Craig is still in there and it's so wonderful when he comes out. He is a loving man and would never have had an affair when my mom was alive and would never have one now, just out of his own ethics and respect for me and my deceased mother. I know that. But the other dad is lonely, unfiltered, and has taken an interest in your mother."

Katy became aware of the sunshine streaming in through the window behind Thomas, and she could feel its warmth. She touched Levi gently on his elbow.

"I think he truly cares for her, Levi. You should see how he acts when they're together. And if I can be a bit presumptuous, I think your mother feels the same way. She seems happy and more responsive when they are together. Maybe God is letting them have each other, in a very unconventional way? This brings up many conflicts in my mind, not the least of which are moral considerations, but I'm not sure this is about sex—though it may well be. I think it's about the companionship both of them need. Perhaps we can give it some time and see how it goes? I honestly feel that God is okay with what's happening."

She could barely believe what she had just said, but said it she had. She felt a weight lift off her shoulders, and she smiled at Levi and Thomas.

Levi had lost his angry expression and taken on the look of a child as he fought back tears. He wanted so much to remain angry but was having a heck of a time. Suddenly, he could hold it back no longer. He couldn't stop the flow of emotions or the tears. How could he agree to such a thing? Thomas got up and sat next to Levi, putting his arm around him. Katy followed suit and sat next to him on his other side.

"I can only imagine what you're feeling, Levi," Thomas said. "The sorrow of her disease and this new situation is overwhelming. I know I shouldn't give advice, but I think Katy is right. Both of them are such good people. Perhaps God is giving them a small measure of peace and comfort together."

Levi stopped crying and looked into Thomas's eyes. "All right," he said. "I'll give it some time and try and find a way to deal with it."

"Would you mind if I prayed, Levi?" Thomas asked.

"I guess it wouldn't hurt."

"God," Thomas began, "you made us all, and we are grateful for your many blessings. I'm thankful that we can come together as friends and as caregivers for Mr. Craig and Miss Betty. We all love them so very much, as we're sure you do. We don't claim to understand this, God, but we know that you know what's best for them. Please guide us as we deal with it, and please help Mr. Craig and Miss Betty to have some form of peace through this, however you have it turn out. Guide us, Lord. In Jesus's name I pray, amen."

Levi looked up as Thomas finished and seemed to be at peace. "I'm not much for religion and all that," he said, "but your prayer and this conversation are meaningful to me. Thanks to you both, and thanks for caring about my mom."

"You are more than welcome, Levi," Thomas said. "Perhaps as things go on here, we can revisit this topic and perhaps have even deeper conversations."

"Okay," replied Levi. "That would be fine."

CHANGES
Tritium (2005)

A t 7:15 a.m. Craig was sitting at his desk with the door closed, contemplating the event, yesterday's HQ briefing, and his life in general. He thought about how he had been distracted by that joke during his discussion with NA-1. *I've got to be more careful,* he thought. *I'm a Swiss watch, not a daydreamer.*

Craig got up at 4:30 each morning, made coffee, had a twenty-minute devotional, then went to the gym, showered, and made it to the office by 7:00. Once there, Craig's first task to prepare for the day was reviewing his planner and the day's calendar, which Claire would have placed on his desk the night before. Inevitably, Craig would mark it up the next morning and give it to her to facilitate the changes.

Claire didn't mind it. She enjoyed working for Craig and the status of her position. She was the Queen Bee. All the other assistants had to show her respect, even the ones with more age and experience. She was proud to be the GM's secretary and ignored the jealousy of others who thought her looks had secured her title. Claire didn't care; in fact, she actually reveled in it. She knew that if she invoked Craig's name, the other assistants had no choice but to do her bidding.

At thirty-five, Claire had been divorced from her high school sweetheart for three years. He had failed to show her the respect she deserved, at least that was her opinion. After divorcing him, she dated sporadically but had no real boyfriend. An avid runner, she lost ten pounds after the split and kept it off. She spent an inordinate amount of her salary on clothes, and she knew she was easily the best-dressed lady in Tritium. She was not promiscuous but extremely attractive, a fact she also knew.

I didn't trust her. I had failed in persuading Craig to select an assistant who was more of a caring matron than a hot babe, so I kept my eye on her constantly. She wore short skirts and sat with her legs crossed, swinging one back and forth with her shoe dangling, which excited Craig but drove me crazy. Hell, it excited me too, but I knew better and did everything I could think of to keep it from arousing Craig.

A knock at the door interrupted Craig. "Come in," he said.

Claire opened the door with a cup of steaming black coffee in her hand. She did her best to be in the office before Craig, knowing he would already have a to-do list ready for her when he arrived. Her routine included starting the coffee and reading emails while she waited for her boss.

"Coffee, sir?"

"Yes, Claire. Thank you, but you know you don't need to bring me coffee. I would never ask you to do that."

Craig knew that doing so would be demeaning. He always hated it when some managers asked their female assistants to get them coffee. Craig had learned how to treat the women who worked for him with respect—at least he thought so. And while he wanted to interact with them just like the males who worked for him, he couldn't quite do that. For example, he never closed the door with a female in his office, except for Claire and Stacy. He totally trusted them both and often discussed very sensitive issues with them from personnel and classification standpoints.

"No worries, sir," Claire responded as she handed Craig the cup. "Are you ready to go over your calendar for the day?"

"Yes, I'm ready. Please have a seat."

She chose the leather chair that was just a few feet in front of Craig's desk. Craig had two chairs there, and an eight-foot rectangular wood conference table that seated six occupied the other side of his office. The federal government had specs for everything from desks, chairs, tables, and computers to nuclear warhead components. DOE also had very strict rules about how contractors used their stuff. Any use of department facilities, computers, etc., for private use was forbidden, especially if any profits were involved. Craig often told his staff that they were more likely to be fired for using their government computer to buy a personal hot tub than for ordering the wrong multimillion-dollar part for a project—and he was serious.

Craig's desk and table were neat and orderly. He was a stickler for appearances. His current work and planner were the only things resting on his desk pad. The remaining space held neat piles of paper. He was old school and kept tidy stacks for each key initiative he was working on. The stack at the right-hand side of his desk was the Tritium release event pile, and he knew every paper in it.

Craig looked down at his calendar. Truthfully, he didn't really feel prepared to discuss the upcoming events for the day.

"Claire," he started, "I need some closed-door time today to get my thoughts together and evaluate the event information. So, first, cancel my eight o'clock meeting with finance. I know it's short notice, but you can explain it to them. Reschedule for next week. Second, I won't be attending the weekly radiation control meeting in the facility. Call Stacy and let her know so she can apologize for me. I think they'll understand, don't you?" Craig asked politely.

"Yes, sir," Claire replied. "You've got a lot on your plate at the moment."

Craig looked up and smiled and noticed for the first time that Claire was wearing a low-cut, V-neck sweater. He looked directly at the bottom of the V. He was mesmerized.

With my help, he suddenly realized what he was doing and looked back at his calendar. His face became hot, and he couldn't regain his focus. I tried to help, but his mind was chaotic. His orderly mind was now suddenly misfiring. Had Claire noticed? Get a hold of yourself, I willed. Come on, man. Recover.

After a short pause, Craig again focused. "I think that's all the changes," he said. "I can keep the rest of my schedule, but I'm going to close my door for at least an hour to look over the release data, then I'll head to the control room to see what's new there."

"Yes, sir," Claire responded as she got up. She walked out of Craig's office, and just as she was closing the door behind her, she smiled. She had caught Craig's gaze, and while she felt a little surprised, she was proud of having done so.

I really couldn't tell what was up with Craig. In the past I felt as though I was battling his software and at times what seemed to be an outside force. However, his discipline and values had always kept his libido in check. And I could almost always immediately divert him with just a few thoughts about his wife, kids, baseball, Jesus, whatever. Not anymore. It was becoming increasingly harder to keep him in line. It was as if I was being blocked out of communication with him.

Craig pulled the Tritium release pile onto his desk pad and began poring through the data, searching for a red flag. He studied the names of the team handling the root cause investigation and examined their plan of attack and initial data. It seemed the spike in pressure preceding the event had been totally unexpected. Apparently, the operator had done everything correctly, but somehow the loading software had taken over and increased the pressure without the operator's command. A sudden fear overwhelmed Craig. He knew what the evidence was telling him, but he refused to believe it just yet. It looked as though Hidebound might be right. Maybe the control system had taken it upon itself to load without operator input, which would create a nightmare.

Craig finished reviewing his pile and then pushed his chair back, stood up, and opened his door. As he walked by Claire, he used every ounce of restraint in his body to avoid looking at her V-neck. He walked through the office suite, down the hall, and out the outer door into the Tritium courtyard. He proceeded through the door and headed into the control room. Tom and Stacy were already there discussing the data on the main facility computer screen. They had pulled up the loading procedure and were going over it step-by-step. Craig knew that his being in the room would affect their discussion, but he couldn't help that. Tom would be especially mindful of Craig's presence.

After a few minutes, it became clear that Tom and Stacy were discussing what Craig had garnered from the data in his office— the apparent, inadvertent, or maybe intentional, spike in pressure that caused the glove box release. It became even more clear that they had halted their discussion once he entered and were now trying to change the subject. Craig seized on the obvious shift in their conversation.

"Relax, everybody! Just relax. I know you were talking about the cause of the spike and you don't need to dance around it now that I'm here. Just continue as if I weren't here. There will be plenty of time to spin this later." He spoke the latter part of his statement softly so that only Tom and Stacy heard it. He knew that his statement would compel Stacy to speak freely but would have no effect on Tom, who would hedge his words no matter what Craig said.

"Thank you, sir," Stacy replied. "We think we've found when and where the event occurred but are still less than positive why. The operator entered the reservoir data, but the computer's loading system did not take it. Instead, it changed the input to a higher number. As of yet, there is no way to explain it. Our computer software folks are working around the clock in Tom's area, trying to come up with a reason."

"Are you sure they are the ones who should be evaluating it?" Craig asked. "Can we be sure they'll be open and objective about a mistake they made?"

Tom looked insulted by the comment. "Of course we can, sir. My folks would never attempt to hide anything," he said forcefully.

"I wasn't trying to besmirch your people, Tom, but it's human nature to protect one's own interests. Believe me, I know," Craig answered sternly.

"Sir, the computer staff in Tom's organization is all we have," Stacy added in an attempt to deescalate the obvious confrontation Craig had initiated. "I mean, really, that's all we have."

Craig was quiet for a minute, waiting for his blood pressure to come down a bit.

"I know we have a great computer staff, but an independent set of eyes would be helpful and show the department that we are introspective. I was thinking about it as I sat in my office this morning. Tom, I want you and Stacy to procure the services of an outside vendor to help with this root cause evaluation. I don't want it to be any of the consultants we used in the recent software upgrade. I need a fresh set of eyes, and those eyes need to be very good."

"That won't be easy, sir," Tom replied. "During the software upgrade, we used all three of our standing purchase order consultants. Getting a new PO issued will take weeks. I'm not sure we can do it."

Craig's blood pressure soared again.

"Bull—!" he shouted, without thinking. "You just don't want one. Stacy, call Fran at corporate. She has a number of POs for software support. She can use one of them, and corporate can pay for it. Tell her we need them tomorrow morning. No excuses. I'll call Dick and let him know we need the support. It will happen. I briefed him on the issue last night but didn't think about support until this morning."

Craig had briefed his corporate boss from home last night. Dick had offered support, but Craig had refused it at that moment.

Seeing the look of shock on their faces, Craig held up one hand. "I'm sorry for the language, you two. It's a trying time, but there is no excuse."

Craig felt hypocritical, since he always scolded facility personnel for using profanity. He hated foul language, stressing to his employees that it wasn't about morality, but professionalism.

I was worried. Here was yet another example of a subtle but startling change in Craig.

Craig made his way back to his office. He felt an increasing sense of dread as he thought about the call he now had to make to his boss. He had sent Dick an email and copy of the Occurrence Reporting and Processing System report filed with DOE, though he had downplayed it. He generally didn't want help from the company, but it was necessary in this case. It was the only way.

Dick was located in DC and managed all the corporate government business. This included the GOCO (Government Company) jobs like Tritium. These contracts were generally lucrative and earned money primarily through subjective contract awards called award fee. These awards are based on DOE's opinion of how the contractor is performing, thus determining how much the contractor makes in profit.

Craig arrived at his office suite and closed the door. Gathering his thoughts, he called Dick's mobile number from the phone on his desk. Cell phones were strictly prohibited inside Tritium for security reasons. It was a royal pain, but with all the classified information inside the facility, a rigid ban was a must. Craig always turned his cell phone off and left it in his truck before coming through the gate.

Craig and Dick had always enjoyed a pleasant, though largely superficial, relationship. Dick had a nuclear engineering degree from Georgia Tech but was a businessman, not an engineer. He didn't try and hide it. He'd say, "I'm a rambling wreck from Georgia Tech, but not much of an engineer." Dick was actually pretty technical and had a business acumen second to none. He was generally pleasant but decisive and at times brutal when events required it. Dick respected Craig as one of the best GMs in the DOE contracting business. He seldom had any major problems and tended to earn more than ninety-five percent of available fees every year, which is what mattered to Dick. It was a well-run contract, and Dick knew it. He chaired Craig's board of directors as a corporate oversight function for the contract. Because he trusted Craig, those meetings were generally much shorter than the other ones Dick chaired.

"Hello," Dick greeted Craig as the call went through.

"Hi, Dick. How's it going?"

"Good. I'm in Carlsbad for a board meeting. What's up, buddy?"

"Well, I'm sure you read the email and ORPS attachment I sent you yesterday. Looks like I may need your help after all."

"Sure. What can I do? Is this release a bigger deal than we thought?"

"No, I don't think so," Craig replied, trying to keep Dick's alarms from sounding. "I think it's all going to be fine, but I do need some corporate response for the root cause analysis team. You know how much DOE likes corporate reach-back." Craig was again downplaying the seriousness of the incident to keep Dick from becoming overly concerned. "DOE will love you for it."

"Not a problem. What do you need?"

"Well, I asked Stacy to call Fran to request two or three of her best computer software people. We want to put them on our root cause team as independent members. Our people will of course be on it, and DOE will oversee it. However, we need some independent eyes to show DOE we're being objective in whatever we find. Oh, and we need at least one of them to be well-versed in artificial intelligence."

"Really?" Dick asked. "Why?"

"It's the latest craze, and DOE wants to be sure that some of the software upgrades we made weren't somehow polluted with AI." Craig realized Dick would eventually learn about the AI issue, so just as well he put it out there now.

"All right," said Dick. "I'll phone Fran as soon as we hang up. I know she's in the DC office because she's joining the board meeting by phone later today."

"Thanks, Dick, and please stress to her that the need is immediate—tomorrow or just as soon as she can get them here. I want to get this over with and get it off DOE's screen. Award Fee ratings will be out in about six weeks, and I definitely want this resolved by then."

"Good point. I'll make it happen, buddy. Keep me posted and let me know if this thing gets worse."

"Will do," Craig responded. "Talk to you soon, and thanks again."

Craig sat back in his chair and stared at the picture hanging on the far wall at the end of his conference table. It was a black-and-white photo of three guys in baseball caps in the mid-'60s watching a ground-level detonation of a warhead at the Nevada Test Site. The three men had their hands on their hips as they stood and stared at the ominous mushroom cloud in the distance. *Those were the days*, he thought. *Hope this AI thing doesn't turn out to be like that.*

When Claire saw the light on her phone go off, indicating that Craig's call had ended, she got up and softly knocked on his door.

"Come in," he said.

Claire opened the door and asked if everything was okay.

"Yeah," said Craig. "I had to call Dick and ask for some corporate support to oversee the root cause team. I need some objective eyes to keep Tom and his engineers from playing 'f—k the truth.'" After Craig said it, he knew he shouldn't have.

I was on full alert! Normally, a profane and sexual metaphor like that would never have come out of his mouth. My God, who is this loose cannon? It took Claire a minute to even grasp what Craig had said.

Claire blushed, totally taken aback, but she managed a smile and said, "Oh, I get it, Craig. I know you hate to bring in corporate support, so this must be really bothering you. Is there anything I can do to help?"

"What did you have in mind?" Craig responded, smiling back.

Oh, no. This isn't over. Craig has to know that the joke was terrible and maybe even considered sexual harassment, and now this? I tried everything I could. I began to relay all sorts of warnings to Craig's brain. I tried to bring back all the disciplined morals he held so dear. I reminded him of how he had given a speech at an all-hands meeting about sexual harassment and it included just this kind of stuff. Wake up, Craig! You're headed for the ditch! It was no use. I wasn't getting through. Craig sat there, leaning back in his chair with an unusually stupid grin on his face.

Claire's blush turned to a full flame. "Um, anything I can do, sir," she responded. "Just let me know." She was a hot mess. Her legs felt weak, and her mind was racing as she spun around to return to her desk.

"I'll keep that offer in mind," Craig said as he watched her walk away. He was totally focused on her muscled calves.

We're doomed. Who is this? The Craig I knew was a good, Christian man who loved his wife and daughter more than anything in the world. He would not cheat on Anne. Ever. Craig's mind was in chaos. To some extent, he knew what he had just done was wrong, but he didn't seem to be able to access the memes in his mind to feel regret. And I wasn't getting through either.

After a brief, mental romp with Claire, Craig's mind returned to a more normal state and to the issue at hand. He stood up and walked to Claire's desk. She was still flushed and shyly looked up as Craig stood in front of her.

"I'm going over to Dr. Oddlove's office to brief him. Goes without saying I'm under a lot of stress right now, Claire, and I'm depending on you for support. Sorry about the comment earlier; guess I should watch that kind of joking."

Craig somehow knew that what he said to Claire was inappropriate, and he awkwardly and halfheartedly tried to correct it. "I'll be back in half an hour or so. See you then."

After Craig left, Claire continued to ponder what had occurred. She'd always had a favorable and professional relationship with him. Craig was the kind of boss she liked working for—he was smart, reliable, disciplined, and funny. Plus, he kept her in the loop on almost everything. She appreciated that Craig wanted her input and support since many managers were less reliant on their assistants. This made her days exciting and the time at the office go by faster. It also meant that she knew much more than the other assistants, and she used that advantage to retain her position. But what just happened? Craig had sexually harassed her. Now what should she do? Should she disclose it to HR in case she needed it later? Should she sit down and discuss it with Craig? Should she tell anyone?

After about fifteen minutes of shock and contemplation, she reached into her purse and pulled out her personal planner, which organized all her non-work-related appointments, thoughts, goals, and other important information. In her notes section, she carefully began to write: Very strange encounter with Craig today. He made an explicit, profane, and sexual joke and then asked me what I had in mind when I offered to help him from a strictly work standpoint.

She reviewed what she'd written, then closed her planner and returned it to her purse.

***

"Come in, Craig," Dr. Oddlove said.

Craig went in and took a seat at the conference table. Dr. Oddlove left his desk and joined Craig at the table.

"I just wanted to give you a short briefing on where we are and our path forward," Craig said. "I was in the facility this morning, and it seems we have a pretty good picture of what happened. The root cause team is doing an excellent job, and I believe they know exactly what happened from a purely objective standpoint. They have chronicled all the operator's actions during the loading operations, and they all look to be fine. However, the control system continued to increase pressure beyond the operator's command. This is obvious from the step-by-step history provided by the system. I mean, there seems to be no operator error involved. And while I guess that's good news, it does raise some perplexing questions, such as, very simply, why?"

Craig had learned over the years to be very open with his local customer. In this case, he was being as open as he could.

"I was afraid of this, Craig," Dr. Oddlove said. "The system somehow took over, didn't it? Maybe Hidebound was right about the AI component of the software upgrade."

"We don't know that yet," Craig said truthfully, "but I share your fear. I also have the fear that my engineering team may be reluctant to find their mistake. I mean, it's only natural. Although we have done everything we know to do to assure that Tritium has a healthy, safety-conscious work environment that allows people to be open and honest without fear of reprisal, human nature may cause them to be defensive."

"I know that, Craig, and believe you're right to be worried. What do you plan to do?"

"Well, I just got off the phone with my boss, Dick. I've asked corporate to send their computer experts here to assess the situation. Those folks will report to me. And getting to your point, I've asked for at least one of them to be an expert in AI. I will meet with them regularly, apart from meetings with engineering and operations, on the root cause to ensure that the truth comes out."

"Excellent," Dr. Oddlove said, smiling at Craig. "Great idea. My folks are watching the team and reporting what they see, so we can compare notes."

Craig agreed. "Got it. We'll get to the bottom of this and fix it."

The relationship between Dr. Oddlove and Craig was unique. Many DOE counterparts saw their job as being that of a hammer to beat the lowly contractor into submission. But Craig and Dr. Oddlove not only shared mutual trust and respect, they also shared a vision to fulfill the Tritium mission for the stockpile and to ensure that Tritium remained the best-run facility in the Weapons Complex.

Dr. Oddlove was SES, or senior executive service, which meant that he too was eligible for an incentive each year and that his salary was fairly high for a government employee. However, being SES brought with it certain risks, as compared to normal GS, or general service, employees of the government. Unlike GS employees, Dr. Oddlove could be fired or reassigned by HQ. Firing a GS employee, even an incompetent one, required an act of God once the employee had made it through the initial probationary period. However, Craig knew that if anyone ever needed to fall on his sword, it would be him, not Dr. Oddlove. It was all part of his job, one that compensated him well. He was fully aware that DOE would always blame him, the contractor, whenever problems and issues arose, and he told his staff as much. "It's the profession we chose and the deal we cut. If you can't live with it, maybe you should sell shoes," Craig had told them more than once.

***

At six-thirty the next morning, Craig—having skipped his usual workout to be in the office early—was at his desk reading emails and growing perturbed. It was too early to be stressed, but the report about the root cause was really just a bunch of technical fluff. As he read it, he received an email from his boss. *Dick's up already and emailing*, Craig thought. *Impressive.* He opened the short email and read that the support he'd requested would be in his office today by nine. He responded back with a hearty thanks and copied Fran and Stacy since they'd both been instrumental in making it happen.

As Craig was reading, he heard Claire come in. She was putting her lunch in the refrigerator in the waiting area and getting set up for the day. Craig suddenly remembered what he said to Claire the day before and was concerned about it, but only slightly. There was also a drive in him to continue the banter.

I was horrified. I had to do something to get him back to himself. Once again, I generated memories of Anne and Katy. I even created a scenario of a sexual harassment lawsuit and tried to run that through his processor. But it was as if my input was shorting to ground. Either he wasn't receiving my input or was disregarding it. Craig had never ignored me before. He had battled me and that supernatural feeling we felt from time to time, but this was different. Craig had become an island I couldn't reach, at least continuously. I began to pray that God would somehow intercede. It didn't seem to work, at least not initially. I could see the mischief in Craig's mind and was helpless to stop it.

Craig got up and walked over to Claire's desk. "Good morning, Claire," he said.

"Good morning."

"How was your evening?"

"Fine," she said, avoiding eye contact. "And yours?"

"Good, I guess. Got up early because once I woke up, my mind went right to the release and what we need to do. Are you ready to plan our day?"

"Yes," she replied. "I'll be right there."

A few minutes later, Claire came in and took her normal seat in front of Craig, her expression serious and professional. Craig began giving directions for the day.

"The team from corporate will be here at nine, so please work with Stacy and Tom first thing to arrange for their temporary IDs. They will need full facility access. Let's start with one month for now, but hopefully, their visit here will be shorter."

"Yes, sir," Claire replied.

"As soon as they're badged in, please have them meet with me alone. That should only take about ten or fifteen minutes. Then have Stacy and Tom join us. Stacy will have no problem waiting to join in, but Tom may not be happy about it. Just tell him those are my wishes. Then smile."

"Got it, sir," she replied, trying not to smile.

"I'm meeting with them alone to make sure they report to me and not Tom, though he will be handling their day-to-day functions. You can guess why that is, right?"

"Right," Claire replied. "You want the corporate folks to tell it like it is."

Craig often shared the reasons behind his decisions with Claire so she could be of more assistance in supporting him. Claire appreciated and used this extra information. When others asked her about Craig's motives, she would simply smile coyly and say, "I guess he has his reasons." Her access to inside information and her smugness over it drove the other assistants crazy, and Claire knew it.

By the time they'd finished reviewing the day's schedule, Craig was staring at Claire, making her uncomfortable. After a long pause, Craig said, "That should do it, Claire. Um, have I told you lately how much ..."

There was an awkward pause that sent the blood rushing to Claire's face and her mind racing.

"... I appreciate your loyalty and fine work?" Craig finished. "That is all for now."

Relieved, Claire returned to her desk.

***

At nine-thirty, Craig returned from walking the engineering department spaces. He loved to just walk around the administrative offices in the morning, almost as much as walking the facilities. Sometimes, he would stop and talk to folks. Other times, he'd head to a conference room, slip into one of the meetings, and sit quietly for fifteen minutes or so. The tone of the meetings always became more formal with his appearance, but it was amazing how much he learned from those short walkabouts.

As he sat at his desk, Claire appeared in the doorway. "The team is here to see you, sir."

"Send them in."

Three young professionals entered Craig's office, two young men and a woman who looked to be in her early forties. Both young men wore khakis and cream-colored golf shirts, and the woman had on blue jeans and a pressed, white blouse.

"Come in," Craig said while standing to greet them. He shook each one's hand and thanked them for coming. "Please have a seat." He motioned to the chairs and closed the door.

He glanced into the waiting area near Claire, who was now back at her desk. No sign of Tom or Stacy. *Good*, he thought. As they sat down, Craig asked if they wanted any coffee or bottled water. All three cordially declined.

"Well, let me first thank all three of you for halting the other important projects you were working on to come and help us here in Aiken. At least the weather is better today—only going to be in the eighties. I know this is an inconvenience for you, but I truly appreciate it," Craig smiled. "Tell me a little about yourselves."

One of the two men started. "I'm David Stone. I've only been with the company for a year, and I mostly worked on software updates for the government sector. Before that, I did programming on contract for a small company in Lansing, Michigan."

The other young man then briefly introduced himself. "I'm Steven Hart and I've got two years' experience with the company, including working on artificial intelligence. I've been primarily assigned to a bid that we're putting together for a job with the Navy. The bid is for oversight of another Navy contractor for AI changes to aircraft software. That's really all I can say about it, given classification concerns."

"That's enough for me. Thanks," Craig said.

Lastly, the woman spoke. "My name is Mary Burns. I've been with the company for over ten years now, and I supervise these two brilliant young men as well as fifteen other software engineers in various contracts and locations. At the moment, you pretty much have our DC software staff on site here," she said in a way that let Craig know she'd reorganized her professional life for him.

"Thank you again for making this sacrifice. Let me get right to it. We will be joined in a few minutes by my operations manager, Stacy Ottly, and my engineering manager, Tom Palisade. As I'm sure you know, we had a major glove box release. Tom and his staff will brief you on the technical details of what exactly happened. Those details will be critical in what I want you to do. Loading tritium reservoirs is our mission here. During the loading process for a batch of reservoirs, we had a significant release. We somehow exceeded pressure. Reading the report this morning from the root cause analysis team, of which you will soon be a part, it seems as though we had a line failure. That is, the excess pressure caused the line to breach.

"But, of course, the engineering analysis of a breakpoint is not your concern," Craig continued. "The mechanical engineers will handle that in excruciating detail. What your focus should be is why our software allowed the system to over-pressurize in the first place. You'll need to re-review the most up-to-date findings on the timing of what happened and who did what.

"I wouldn't normally start with this for fear of prejudicing your opinions, but I feel I must. This fall we upgraded our software systems with a short outage. Since then, we've worked out a few minor bugs, but this event is the first real problem since the upgrade, and it's a doozy. As part of the upgrade, engineering convinced me and the department to include a learning function. I tried hard to understand all the aspects but am pretty sure I didn't. I was told that this learning function was benign but would be very helpful in understanding our data and in coming up with cost-effective approaches to improve efficiency. The department was skeptical of the function, but after days of computer lingo discussions, we all agreed with engineering to go ahead with the learning function.

"Now, in full disclosure, the department and I are concerned that this function may have played a part in the over-pressurization. That's about as blunt as I can be. Your mission is to resolve the issue. You are to have no fear of what your findings are. I want the truth and the whole truth, no matter what it is. That will be between you all and me. From there, I will decide where to take it and what to do about it. If you feel any pressure whatsoever from engineering, operations, or anyone else to sugarcoat your findings, you are to come directly to me, and I'll deal with it. You are also to keep any revelations to yourself until you've first told me. Of course, you will have to work with Tom and his engineers and that will require cooperation, but the outcome is to be reported to me first. I know that may prove to be uncomfortable for you, but it's got to be that way. Any questions?"

The three of them seemed a bit taken aback by what Craig had just said and looked questioningly at each other, especially at Mary.

After a pause, she said, "Well, we love a challenge. Sounds like a political minefield, but I think we're up to it."

Shortly thereafter, Stacy and Tom joined the others at the table, and Craig went through the obligatory introductions. He then gave a somewhat more benign description of the task ahead. He wanted to let the thing play out and see if his suspicions about the AI upgrade and his intuition about Tom being parochial were both true. Time would tell.

LOGIC
Fall Leaves (2013)

Shortly after five on Friday evening, Katy was closing up shop early to stop by and see her dad before starting the weekend. Visiting him always flooded her with mixed emotions. There was the dead time, the smells, the caregivers, and, of course, Betty. Nevertheless, Katy loved her dad and visited him out of both love and duty. She needed to fulfill her responsibility, no matter how painful.

She hoisted her cherished attaché to her shoulder. It was a beige glove leather bag she used to take work home, a gift from Craig when she first started practicing law. It reminded her of the relief she felt and the pride her parents felt when she passed the bar.

Katy walked out of her office into the waiting area and stood in front of her assistant, who was organizing papers on her desk and preparing to leave for the weekend too. The waiting area was very nice but designed for functionality with just two leather couches and a leather chair surrounding a glass-top table with magazines organized neatly on top. The area served Katy and two other lawyers.

"I've got the discovery from the UPS case and will review it over the weekend," Katy called out to her assistant. "I'll draft up a summary and send it to you on Sunday. Please don't feel the need to come in on Sunday to edit it for distribution to the partners. It can wait until Monday morning. I'd like to get it to them by COB Monday to review for the partners' meeting on Tuesday. I don't want them to get it too early, or they'll be sending me questions before we meet," she added, smiling at her as she turned to leave.

"Got it," her assistant said. "Good plan."

***

Katy walked into Emerald Hall and saw Craig, Betty, and Olga seated at their normal table; Levi occupied the fourth chair. He was sitting quietly and staring at his cell phone while the others ate their dinners. No one noticed Katy until she arrived at the table.

"Hey, Dad," she said in as cheerful a voice as she could muster. "How are you doing today?"

Craig looked up and smiled, his brain firing in a pleasant way. "Oh, it's my beautiful, brilliant, take-no-prisoners, lawyer daughter. Isn't she beautiful?"

"Thanks, Dad. How are you doing, Betty?"

Betty just looked up emotionlessly. She didn't recognize Katy but felt no concern. Katy seemed pleasant enough, but Betty sensed no significance or connection to her.

"Hi, Levi," Katy added, nodding to him. "Good to see you. Mind if I pull up a chair?"

At this, Levi put down his phone and smiled at Katy. "Hey, Katy. Of course, please sit with us."

A friendship had begun to sprout as Levi slowly came to terms with the relationship between his mother and the old man at the table. His mother indeed seemed happy, peaceful, and content. Levi and Katy now talked at least once a week, when their visits coincided, and they'd shared a number of long conversations. Thomas was often a part of their new, informal, and impromptu support group. Though generally very even tempered, Levi was a strong-willed young man, one who would never admit to needing or attending an actual support group. At six-foot-seven and possessing what could be an imposing physique, he was too self-reliant for that, but deep down he knew the time spent with Katy and Thomas was good for him.

"How's it going, Levi?"

"Pretty good, I guess," he replied, shrugging. "I just got here ten minutes ago myself, and they were already at the table."

Both Katy and Levi tended to plan their visits around meals. It was by far the best time to visit in that their common focus—food—mitigated the uncomfortable silences. The few times Levi had visited Craig and Betty in Craig's room had been unbearable. Unlike Katy, Levi would never enter Craig's room when there was a potential of seeing his mother in bed with Craig. Never.

Levi and Katy made small talk for a few minutes.

"I was here on Tuesday and stayed until after dinner. As always, Mom and your dad were the last to finish. As they headed to your dad's room, I walked to the nurses' station to ask a question about Mom's meds. As I got there, one of the residents—actually it's that lady over there with the short red hair—was irate," he said, nodding inconspicuously to a far table. "She had this horrified look in her eyes and kept asking where her husband was. 'I need to talk to my husband!' she was shouting. I backed off and watched as the nurse tried to calm her down. Finally, she turned to walk away and noticed me standing there. She told me she must talk to her husband. It was urgent. I didn't know what to do, so I just said I'd try to contact him and asked her for his name and phone number. She frowned at me, paused, then said, 'You see, that's the problem. I don't know his name. Can you help me?' I told her I'd try and get in touch with him and tell him she needed to see him immediately. She seemed to buy it and thanked me for the assistance before walking off to what I guess is her room."

Katy gave a short laugh. "Wow, Levi, you may be able to get a part-time job here. You're becoming as good as Thomas."

They smiled at each other.

"This place really becomes a cuckoo's nest after dinner," Levi said, but then he immediately regretted his comment and apologized.

"Oh, no need for that, Levi," Katy said. "Legally speaking, the truth is a perfect defense. It does remind me of the movie *One Flew Over the Cuckoo's Nest* at times too. While it's all so tragic, sometimes you just can't help but laugh. It can help."

Katy continued, "One night when I was here before Betty and Dad became friends, I was standing in the hall in front of Dad's room when a resident came up and asked me for the code, claiming she had to get out. It was the only time I can remember anyone here even realizing they were locked in. She continued to tell me that she'd simply come here for dinner, but the staff wouldn't let her out. She told me she lived just a few blocks away, but now she was trapped. They were making her spend the night. Told me she'd never come for dinner here again! In the middle of her rant, a male resident from down the hall came out to see what was going on. The lady asked him if he was spending the night there. He vehemently shook his head, claimed he was heading home, then together they angrily set off toward the nurses' station."

They both laughed.

"I didn't handle it nearly as well as you, Levi. You may have the gift," Katy said.

Betty, Craig, and Olga paid no attention to the conversation between Katy and Levi. They just kept eating. Craig was mindful of Levi's presence and still felt a little afraid and jealous whenever he came to visit.

I was grateful. I gladly welcomed any mitigating force that might keep Craig from acting up.

Levi had become comfortable around Katy. Though she was intelligent and beautiful, he was drawn to her because of her insight and the way she made him feel calm and at ease.

"Do you have a few minutes to talk in private?" he asked.

"Sure," said Katy. "Let's go to the waiting area in front of Dad's room so we can see when they finish eating and head back that way."

A few minutes later, seated in the leather chairs facing each other, Katy asked, "What is it, Levi?"

"Well, I've been thinking a lot about all this, especially about that time Thomas, you, and I prayed together. It's been eating at me ever since. I know you're a religious person. Would it be okay if I ask you a few pointed questions?"

"Sure," said Katy. "I'm certainly no expert when it comes to faith, but I'll try my best to answer your questions."

"This whole God thing has never meant much to me," Levi said. "I attended church as a kid, but it just never made sense. So, I just dismissed the whole concept and went on with my life. Now, suddenly I feel the need to reevaluate my opinion. That night we prayed really has stayed with me. I can't shake the feeling. But as I think about it logically, it seems circular and silly to me to be praying about this situation to a god who created the whole mess in the first place. I mean, logic says this all-knowing, all-powerful god guy who knows the past, present, and future caused this to happen to my mother. Right? And you believe he wants us to pray about it. So, he caused it, might cure it, and yet all the time knows what will happen anyway. The whole thing seems like illogical nonsense to me. I hope I haven't offended you with this, but you're the only one I could talk to. It's been driving me crazy. I'm not sure why I'm so focused on this, but I can't seem to get it off my mind. Something in my head won't let me drop it. Maybe I'm losing it."

Levi's speech caused Katy's brain to go into mega spark, like there was a multi-person conference call in her head and everyone was talking at the same time. She recalled memories of Sunday school, discussions with her dad, and long talks with Grandpa Al about predestination and other theological topics. Katy looked at Levi and smiled.

"Levi, you are asking the questions that philosophers and clergy have wrestled with throughout time. Heady stuff; you're obviously smarter than you look! Just kidding!" she said, trying to add a bit of humor to lighten the heavy look on Levi's face. It worked. He smiled back at her knowingly.

"I've wrestled with the same concepts, Levi. Folks like you and I can't help it. Our reasoning skills won't let us simply accept things that make no sense logically. I have spent a good bit of time coming to terms with what I believe and why I believe it. If you want, I can walk you through my thoughts on the subjects you brought up, but they're just that, my thoughts."

"Please do," Levi replied.

"Well, let me start with what I think is the pillar of my beliefs: faith. Faith doesn't come easy, but God loves it. The Bible is full of faith examples—He loves when we accept Him by faith. It's kind of like God's currency. All the heroes in the Bible had faith. From Abraham to David to Paul. I'll come back to this later, but keep it in mind. Regarding God's foreknowledge, or predestination— or fatalism, as the scientific community calls it—my Grandpa Al had a theory, which I've embraced. It came to me by way of my dad. It goes something like this. There are only two possibilities, according to my grandpa. He called them the Milestone Theory and the Headbanger Theory, and some of his thoughts were similar to the ones you're having. If He is so good, how could God start all this bad stuff in motion, knowing the end result all along? My grandpa's pastor would say that God knew but didn't predestine it, which drove Grandpa insane. 'No way,' he would say. "If God knew what would happen, then flung it into reality, it was predestined.' He believed foreknowledge and predestination were one and the same.

"What Grandpa believed was that God set the world in motion for His own pleasure and could control it if it got out of hand, but He just let it play out. He gave man true free will. People were allowed to decide for themselves what they would do or not do, and God could intervene as He saw fit. Grandpa would say it's the only explanation that makes sense. God could have planned every detail, but if He did, we would essentially be robots, and what pleasure would that be for God?

He'd be watching a rerun. Grandpa acknowledged how illogical it seemed to pray if events were predestined. He'd ask several key questions: Why had Jesus, the son of God, prayed to not have to die on the cross if it was all predestined? How did God feel bad or angry when things happened that He knew were going to happen? Did God get sad or angry when watching a rerun? He wondered how he could effectively witness to others about Jesus with such an obvious logic flaw.

But Grandpa felt that certain things were, in fact, predestined—certain things like the second coming of Jesus and the eventual Judgment Day. He felt that some events had always been predestined and others were added. He called these predestined events Milestones, and they were going to occur because God said so. The other stuff just played itself out with God intervening as he saw fit.

"But Grandpa was smart enough to know that he may not have it right, though he was pretty sure he did. He was kind of a cocky guy. So, he created what he called his alternate theory, the Headbanger Theory. This concept accomplished two things. First, it was a hedge to his bet that his theory was right. It gave the predestined folks a way out, at least a potential way out. I think it also was a way for Grandpa to appear humble by saying that he may be wrong and who was he to figure out God? He named it Headbanger because trying to figure out this question of the ages was like banging your head against a wall. Since you really couldn't, you might as well stop trying.

Perhaps mankind isn't capable of fully understanding time, creating a flaw in his Milestone Theory. He was actually pretty comfortable with this theory, but Headbanger was not predestination. While in debate about the subject, he'd allow others to reject his Milestone Theory if they were truly Headbangers, but he couldn't let the Predestined-ers off the hook. To him, predestination was a fatal flaw in one's ability to witness about Christ.

"Am I boring you?" Katy asked.

"Heck no! I'm following your every word," Levi said. "You're obviously smarter than you look too."

Katy smiled. "Touché."

"I need some time to think. It seems to make sense, but I need to ponder it."

"Well, take your time. It's pretty heady stuff, but the key, at least to me, is my faith. And that's why I started with that. Regardless of how you come out on all this, you need faith. In the end, that's what it's really about. Faith. For example, I'm not sure whether I believe in the Big Bang or not, but whether I do or don't, my view still requires faith. The two options are that God created everything or that there is no God and at the beginning of time there was this infinitely dense and infinitely small clump of stuff that exploded and formed the universe, the world, and eventually life. The bottom line is that both theories require faith, though scientists don't call it that. They call it a singularity. But either way, there is no way of knowing where the ball of dobadium came from, and there is no way to know where God came from. For me, it's a no-brainer. I'm going with God. It just makes so much more sense from a probability and logistics standpoint. But again, the requirement of faith is unavoidable either way."

"You really have given this stuff a lot of thought, haven't you?"

"I guess I felt I had to," she said. "And having my dad and grandpa droning on gave me no choice."

"Ha," Levi said. "Okay, I have one last question for you."

"Sure," said Katy with a wink, "but remember how dumb I look."

"Assuming everything you said is right, God set this whole thing up and then let it go. Let's assume He wants us to live by His moral code, wants us to believe in Him and His son Jesus, and He wants us to have faith. Let's start with that. But if so, why doesn't He heal my mom and your dad? Seriously, your dad was a good Christian, and my mom was the best woman I've ever known. Why did God let this happen? Why is there so much sorrow and pain in the world, Katy?"

"Man, you ask some doozies!" Katy said, and laughed. "That's another of the timeless questions, one that both my dad and I struggled with. Here is the best I can come up with. It's not a pretty answer and sounds harsh to me, though it's what I believe. Ready? This could hurt."

"Fire away," Levi said.

"Well, the pain we experience on Earth is real and traumatic. People suffer. War, famine, sickness, death. Even Jesus felt pain from this broken world. He wept when he saw Mary crying about Lazarus. However—prepare yourself for this, Levi. Here's the thing. If you have faith in God, and accept his Son as your Savior, then you can be certain you will be with Him for all eternity. Eternity is very, very long and hard to comprehend. I believe we're put here on Earth as a test, and it's that test that's important, despite how briefly we're here. You have this one shot at eternity with Him. Now, if you compare the time on Earth to eternity, it's so small that it's essentially zero. All this pain and suffering lasts for such a short time in view of eternity, it becomes moot by comparison for those who come to know Jesus.

Now, I know that may sound callous, so I share it gingerly. How can anyone think that child molestation or murder or dementia is moot? I certainly don't, at least while we're here on Earth, but the only hope I have, and I do have that hope and belief, is that when I leave this Earth and begin eternity, all pain and suffering will be gone and forgotten. The trip will have been worth it. But please don't think I'm saying your mom's or my dad's dementia isn't significant and heartbreaking. It is."

They were both silent for a moment. "Again, Levi, I apologize for how this may sound to you. I seldom share my thoughts on this, even when people ask. I am always hesitant to go there, but ask you did and it's the best I can do with this perplexing question."

Levi sat back in his chair, staring into space and rubbing his chin. As they sat for another moment in silence, Katy silently prayed. *Jesus, I'm so sorry if I took this too far. I just felt I needed to share my thoughts with Levi. Please send your Holy Spirit now to comfort him, and please don't let what I said hinder in any way the relationship I know you want with him.*

With a somber look, Levi finally spoke. "I get what you're saying, but it troubles me a bit."

"Me too," said Katy. "But it's all I've got." At that moment, she saw Thomas walking toward them. *Awesome*, she thought. *Here comes the cavalry to help.*

"Hey, Thomas," Katy called out.

"Hey there, how y'all doing?"

"Good, I guess. We were just trying to answer the great philosophical questions of the ages," Levi replied.

"No kidding! Sorry I missed that. I could use some answers."

"Katy was nice enough to give me her obviously well-thought-out views," Levi said. "It's a lot to think about, but as I told her, I've been thinking often about the prayer we had together when we were discussing the relationship between our parents. I can't shake the thoughts."

"Hmm," said Thomas. "Maybe God is talking to you, Levi, and I can't think of a better or smarter person to discuss those thoughts with than Katy. I won't ask y'all to rehash all of it now, because I know you both need to leave soon and I need to get things set up for seated calisthenics. Mr. Craig and Miss Betty love it, by the way. But I would enjoy being a part of any future talks if the timing works out. I'm sure we can all learn from each other."

"I'd like that, Thomas," said Levi.

"So would I," Katy added.

Before Thomas left the room, they all agreed to mull over a time and place for their future meeting of the minds. Then Levi thanked Katy once again. As they both stood up, Katy walked over to Levi and hugged him. Even though he wasn't big on hugging, Levi hugged her back. "We'll get through this, Levi," she said. "It's nice to have you as a friend now to help me deal with it."

They both headed for the exit door but stopped by their parents' table. Craig had finished and was watching Betty eat her last few bites, almost as if he was making sure she cleaned her plate. A peaceful look had replaced the confused expression he usually wore. This wasn't lost on either Katy or Levi.

Their farewells went smoothly, unlike many others that were sorrowful. Katy toyed with the idea of telling Levi of her thoughts about David and the virgin but quickly decided against it. Levi had more than enough to think about for the next few days. They left the building together and headed to the parking lot.

COUNTDOWN
Tritium (2005)

Shortly before eight on Friday morning, Craig sat at his desk waiting for the corporate computer folks to arrive. They'd been working with engineering for five full days, and he'd asked for a first briefing from them. He was feeling overwhelmed. The situation at work alone was bad enough, but last night he'd learned that Anne had felt a lump in her breast. Visibly shaken and tearful, she had shown him after he got home. He had done everything he could to reassure her that it was likely nothing, but he urged her to see her doctor the next day. Then they prayed about it together.

Anne was his rock. They had been together since high school. While attending different colleges, they remained a dedicated couple through those years. Anne was intelligent and beautiful and always wanted to be a stay-at-home mom, despite her career potential. When Katy was born, Anne quit work and fully embraced being a traditional housewife and mother. She was the manager of the house and all business related to it, and Craig truly appreciated everything she did, which allowed him to focus on his career. He could leave home early and come home late without worrying about picking up Katy from school or running errands. Anne had it all covered, and her role was invaluable to him.

If that lump turned out to be something serious, he wasn't sure he could go on without her. He'd be lost.

I was glad that Craig felt this way. What I'd seen from him lately concerned me, made me think some of his love for Anne was dissipating, so I urged Craig to pray for her and her doctor's appointment.

Craig looked up to see Claire standing in his doorway. "The corporate team is here to meet with you."

"Send them in," Craig replied.

The team came in quietly and sat at the conference table with Craig.

"Coffee?" Craig asked. They all declined. "Well, what have you learned?"

David and Steven looked at Mary Burns, their supervisor, but said nothing. Mary took the lead.

"I'll let you know what we've found so far, Craig, but I want you both to feel free to join in whenever you want," she said, looking at her two staffers.

"We are now much more familiar with your operations here, and the engineering folks have been very cooperative. All three of us are impressed with the entire root cause team. They're smart people and really know the facility."

Craig smiled but said nothing.

"The DOE facility rep has even been pleasant and easy to work with, though I'm sure he's taking notes for his briefings with your counterpart, Dr. Oddlove, that he's not sharing with us."

"That's to be expected," Craig said, stirring sugar into his coffee.

"We have gone over the events surrounding the release and have not encountered any lack of candor by engineering or operations. The events essentially speak for themselves. What happened is all clearly documented in the computer transaction log and in the shift log written by the shift manager."

Mary shifted in her seat. "Once we got the feel for what did happen, we turned to why," she said. "We really only started this part of our assessment yesterday because we wanted to be sure we understood the technical details of the event."

"Good," replied Craig. "I'm glad we agree on the facts, which I expected. I know it's still very early, but have you come up with any specifics on why it happened?"

"Nothing we're ready to report with certainty yet. We are now combing through the software upgrade package that was installed. It seems to be a well-designed package that the facility system accepted without incident. There were a few error messages during the upgrade that we are evaluating, but nothing looks like a huge issue."

"How about the AI component?" Craig asked. "Have you seen that yet?"

"Well, we have seen it, and it is part of what we are combing through. It looks to be primarily focused toward facility efficiency. It records data, analyzes it, and can make suggestions for improvement. On its face, it looks to be a fairly sound approach. However, as always, the devil is in the details, and we won't know how good or bad it was until we've finished reviewing it."

Steven, the AI expert at the table, then chimed in. "Yes, it does look fairly sound, but we always worry about how the software is programmed to deal with what it analyzes or learns. That's where the trouble can begin. If it simply reports what it is finding, it's generally not a problem. However, if the software in any way allows the analysis to be used without operator input, that can cause a bad day for a facility like this."

"How long will it take to analyze it?" Craig asked.

"Maybe three or four days," Mary replied. "We're not going home this weekend, so we should have more for you by Tuesday or Wednesday."

"Okay," Craig said. "Again, I truly appreciate y'all being here. Please remember that time is of the essence. I want you to take as much time as you need to be sure, but our facility is now down. We aren't doing any meaningful maintenance, and our shipment dates are backing up. We need to get back into operations as soon as possible. I don't say that to rush you, just to let you know the situation."

"I understand," Mary said, standing up and cueing her staff to do the same. "Just as soon as we're ready, I'll get with your assistant to set up a meeting."

Craig offered his thanks once again and escorted the group out his door. Wanting to keep Dr. Oddlove in the loop, Craig immediately phoned his office and briefed him on what the team found. After Craig finished, he asked Dr. Oddlove if Hidebound mentioned anything interesting to him in his briefings.

"Not really," Dr. Oddlove replied. "Our stories seem to be consistent. However, in a related matter, I am very concerned about the effect this release is having on both maintenance and shipments. Tritium has never missed a stockpile shipment. Never. I'm sitting here looking at our logo on the Tritium sign outside my window. It says "Tritium, Never Missed a Shipment." I'd hate to be the first Tritium director to ruin that perfect record, Craig, and I'm sure you feel that way from a contractor's perspective."

Craig noticed a subtle change in Dr. Oddlove's tone. It was a bit condescending, and he wasn't accustomed to it.

"That's for sure," Craig replied. "We won't let that happen, sir."

After hanging up, Craig's mind spun out of control. His consciousness was having a hard time staying on one topic. First, he thought about what a missed shipment, not to mention the award fee reduction, would mean to his career. He then imagined

Anne, crying as the doctor told her she had cancer. He thought about having an affair with Claire if Anne passed.

Stop it, I commanded. How dare you think of Claire like that as Anne is going through this horrifying experience! I was able to steer his thoughts away from Claire, but just barely. Was it the stress getting to him, or was he really losing it? Sure seemed he was losing it, and fast.

As the workday drew to an end, Craig sat at his desk responding to emails, which was usually his last task before leaving the office. He chose to be one of the last to leave the facility each night in case one of his staff needed to stop by and talk about something. It was a courteous thing to do and showed that he was available when needed.

It suddenly dawned on him that he hadn't heard from Anne. He immediately felt guilty for not phoning after her appointment. How could he have forgotten such an important thing? He picked up the phone and called home. Anne answered with what Craig recognized as her quiet voice. This usually meant that he had either forgotten something important, like today, or that she was worried about something; again, like today.

"How'd it go today?" he asked.

After a pause, Anne replied, "Okay, I guess. The biopsy is done. Now we wait."

"Did it hurt? I bet you're sore."

"That's putting it lightly."

"Oh, I'm sorry, babe. I'm sorry that you have to go through this, but I'm praying that it all comes back negative. I truly believe it will."

Craig had prayed for Anne this morning, but to me he didn't seem concerned enough. Not only was he acting erratically, he was growing cold, as if he didn't care as much anymore.

"I'm leaving soon, sweetheart. I'll be home by seven. Should I pick up something for us to eat?" he asked, trying to make amends. "I know you probably don't feel like cooking tonight."

"No," she said. "I made a roast; needed to keep busy this afternoon."

"Okay. See you soon. Love you."

"Love you too."

***

At noon the following Tuesday, Craig again sat waiting for the corporate team to come in and brief him. He had just finished going over the maintenance backlog report. It was staggering and made clear that a full-blown, week-long maintenance outage would occur before operations could begin. If he didn't get the facility up and running, he would miss shipments. To make matters worse, there were rumors the HQ zealots were going to require an Operations Readiness Review prior to restart. DOE could mandate those reviews whenever a facility had an occurrence so critical in nature that it put in question the overall quality of the operations. Those reviews could go on forever, Craig knew, with gray beard consultants, causal analysis, findings, corrective actions, and on and on. It was blasphemy to Craig. Tritium was the star of the Weapons Complex. Those sorts of reviews were for troubled operations, not Tritium. He made that point to Dr. Oddlove. And while the doctor seemed to agree somewhat, Craig noticed just a hint of the condescending tone he'd heard before while talking about missed shipments.

Craig felt truly alone at his desk. Not only was all this happening at Tritium, but today was the day Anne would get the biopsy results. Craig had offered to stay home, but Anne said it wasn't necessary. She knew what Craig was dealing with at work, and she would manage. He felt terrible that he hadn't insisted on being there with her, but he chose work. He began to pray about her results but couldn't really focus. Again, his mind was a jumble of thoughts he was having a hard time grasping.

"The team is here, sir," Claire said from his doorway.

They sat at Craig's table and exchanged the requisite pleasantries until Craig motioned for Mary to begin.

"Well," she said, "we've made it through all the software in the upgrade. All of it, at least once, but we've gone over the AI component several times to be more certain of our results before briefing you."

Mary waited for a response from Craig, but he sat quietly waiting.

"Nothing has changed from our last briefing regarding the software upgrade in general. We now understand it better, and it is, in fact, a high-grade software package. The errors generated during upload were mostly input and assumption errors and were easily fixed."

"What about the AI component?" Craig asked, unable to wait any longer.

"Well, that story isn't quite as good; in fact, it's not good at all. It appears to us as if a key logic error was made in the AI component of the reservoir loading section of the upgrade. The upgrade was designed to take information from actual loading operations and evaluate it. It looked at and kept track of operational data. It did a very good job of collecting all pertinent data as it was designed to do. It then was designed to review that data in various groupings. For example, in a given run, it might collect the line pressure and compare it to vessel pressure and compare that to timing needed to prepare for the weld, given all the checks required by your procedures. Its goal was to collect and compare these various parameters and then use any one of a number of algorithms that had been programmed in to come up with suggestions for the operator."

Mary took a deep breath and glanced at her team. "There were really two main problems," she continued. "First, engineering didn't make the pauses special or critical in the program. As you know, Craig, these pauses are required and are meant to be a final seal of quality, but they can take a while. The AI program quickly picked up on the operational inefficiency.

"The second problem is even bigger than the first. Most of the AI components of the software upgrade were fine. They simply generated reports suggesting tweaks and changes. That's how the software was supposed to work. However, for loading, instead of just generating reports, the programmers went farther. Here, they allowed the software to make minor modifications to itself to tweak operations while still generating the reports like the other operational sections. What the software was trying to do was be efficient. What we think happened was that it had generated numerous reports telling operations and engineering that the pauses were killing your efficiency. It then recommended changes to your procedures like ignoring stupid pauses because history has shown that they essentially never resulted in any needed corrective action. It was telling your troops how good they were and that they could safely operate without them.

"Unfortunately, your folks ignored these reports. They knew there was no way to get around the pauses and they really didn't understand this function well enough to reprogram it. What happened next is what caused your release. The software then tweaked itself to allow the operator to eliminate the pause. This is key. It did not eliminate the pause but instead created a path around the pause that the operator could use. It then notified your folks through endless reports it was generating that it had done so, just as it had been programmed to do. Again, your folks, unfortunately, weren't really reading these reports daily, but were just skimming them. The copious reports numbed your folks, and, as you know, that's a bad thing. In addition, when they did read the reports, they didn't always understand what they were reading, especially the AI sections."

"So, if this software didn't eliminate the pause and didn't take over, how did the release happen?" Craig asked.

"Great question. As I said, the software created a path around the pause, but the operator had to deliberately take that path. And that he did. I would have to say that he deliberately took an abnormal path without really understanding where that path led. The operator was working his way through the loading procedure when he noticed that the pressure was too low, so he began to manually raise it. As he did, he got a message that he didn't fully understand. It told him that he could opt into the auto mode by entering his desired pressure. He did just that, but shouldn't have, per procedure, because the pause was coming up. The software then became giddy with having been given the auto command and took over. It commenced to over-pressurize the system because it didn't recognize that the pause had ordered an operator to close the next valve downstream. It just kept trying to raise the pressure, and she blew. Really just that simple."

Craig turned pale as he processed what he had just heard. His mind quickly reverted to summary mode. What he had just heard was horrific. He had approved a software upgrade that had caused a massive release. His folks were ignoring critical reports that could have prevented it from happening. His folks were ill-equipped to understand the reports and act on them even if they'd read them. It was a nightmare.

"How sure are you that you're right on this?" Craig asked.

"Totally," chimed Steven. "I mean, it's straightforward and obvious, dude."

Mary winced at the way he had addressed Craig. Steven was new, young, and untrained in respecting a guy like Craig, but he was smart as heck and to him it was straightforward. Craig frowned.

"Who knows your opinions?"

"No one, sir," Mary said quickly, trying to take the floor back from Steven. "We wanted you to know first."

"Engineering doesn't even know?"

"No, not really. They know about the reports and what the AI component was telling them, but they haven't put the pieces together yet. How shall I proceed, Craig?"

Craig thought for a moment and then said, "Well, if it's true, it's true. Sit down with Tom and Stacy and go over your findings with them. Once you're through, give me a call and let me know how they took it and what they plan to do about it. I'll meet with them after I get your call. I don't mean to be sneaky here, but I know I have a problem in my software. I need to know if I have a problem in management as well."

"Will do," Mary said as she stood up and led her two staff members out of Craig's office.

Craig tried to make sense of it all but was having a hard time and fearing the briefing he needed to make to Dr. Oddlove. However, he was also afraid that his customer would learn it from Hidebound, and that would be even worse. He walked out to Claire, who was sitting at her desk looking very concerned.

"Is it bad, Craig?" she asked. Claire was bright and knew about the issue and what it might mean to Tritium, to Craig, and, even more importantly, to her.

"It's not good," Craig replied. "I'm going to head over to talk this over with Dr. Oddlove."

"Yes, sir," she replied, looking up to meet Craig's eyes, but they were focused on the cleavage the three opened buttons at the top of her blouse revealed. She began to blush and felt uncomfortable, thankful that Craig was leaving the office. His unusual behavior was putting her on edge.

A few minutes later, Craig walked straight into Dr. Oddlove's office, which was highly unusual, but the circumstance was highly unusual as well.

"Got a minute?" Craig said.

"Sure, Craig. Have a seat."

"I'm here to update you on the event cause. As always, I want you to know what I know."

"Go on," said Dr. Oddlove.

"The good news is that the software package we uploaded was good. The corporate team went over how well-prepared the software had been and how good the installation was. They were very complimentary of our folks, the DOE folks who were involved in it, and of those on the root cause team."

"That's nice, Craig, but get to the bad news, as I have a feeling that's why you're here."

Craig was having a hard time assembling the story in his mind. Normally, he would just dive in, and his brain would form the story and make modifications as he spoke, based on the verbal and nonverbal feedback from his audience. Craig was a master at it. Typically, he could adjust his tone, pace, information, and facial expressions with ease, based on his listener's reception. But today he had no confidence that he would be able to perform as usual, and he wasn't sure why.

"To be blunt, it does appear that the AI section of the new loading procedure could have a perceived flaw."

"Perceived?" Dr. Oddlove asked sarcastically.

Craig was thrown by his tone and tried to recover.

"Um, I say perceived because I think the package was fine, but it may have contributed to an operator error." This wasn't like Craig, who was taking the customer down a path that led to operator blame, which would mitigate his and Tritium's culpability. Only problem was, no review team ever fully blamed an operator. There was always some contributing factor that made the operator screw up.

Craig went on: "The AI components of the software upgrades for all our processes had a sort of 'lessons learned' function that used algorithms to analyze the data it collected to then generate reports that made suggestions to improve efficiency or safety. It was a sound approach."

"I know all that. Get to the point." Dr. Oddlove was growing impatient, and Craig felt his face growing hot. He knew he was losing his customer's trust.

I could do nothing but sit back and watch it unfold. I tried to calm Craig with prayer, to no avail.

"For the loading software, the AI component was a little more advanced. It not only reported the data and made suggestions in the report, but it actually made procedural changes in the software program that could improve efficiency."

"You're kidding," Dr. Oddlove said, immediately understanding the potential issue.

"Well, it's not as bad as it sounds," Craig continued. "It didn't take over the loading or anything like that, but it did allow the operator to deviate from procedures and make a mistake," he said again, trying to steer toward an operator error. "The AI component of the loading software somehow became infatuated on the inefficiencies in our pauses—you know the points where we hold as a final check."

"I sure do," said Dr. Oddlove. "Those pauses are mandatory."

"Right," said Craig. "And our operations folks hold them as sacred. However, after reporting on the inefficiencies of the pauses, the software created a recommended solution for the operator to use to avoid them."

"Wow," said Dr. Oddlove. "We're headed for the ditch, aren't we, Craig?"

"Maybe not; let me finish."

Craig was getting testy too, which was not his normal approach. He was never short-fused with Dr. Oddlove, but he couldn't seem to control it.

"As designed and approved by all of us, including DOE, the program tried to cure the pause inefficiency by giving the operator the option of going into auto mode, a mode it had created. He should have immediately stopped, as this was outside the procedure and his training. Instead, he put his desired pressure into the new auto mode and watched. The system then kept adding pressure until a fitting blew out, causing the glove box release."

"Holy hell, Craig. That's a lot to digest, but let me summarize what I just heard. Your folks added a very dangerous AI component to loading software that allowed this rogue program to change our loading procedures, unchecked, and set the operator up for a disaster, which, in fact, occurred. Further, your folks ignored the initial reports and just let it happen. And finally, you're now trying to blame the poor operator and DOE. Do I have it right?" Dr. Oddlove asked, raising his eyebrows like a sinister villain in a B movie.

We were dead. Craig would never have gone down this path in the past. He would have started with an admission first to disarm the customer. He would have then repented and walked through how they would fix it. He would have told Dr. Oddlove that he would personally call HQ and fall on his sword. That would have worked, but this wasn't the same Craig. I didn't know who it was. His mind had changed into someone else, and I didn't like whoever it was. This new Craig was dumb, self-centered, lewd, and unfiltered.

"I'm not trying to blame anyone," Craig replied forcefully. "Just stating facts. I know we will need to brief HQ, but the information I just gave you is brand new and hasn't been vetted through operations or engineering yet. It's just initial information from the corporate team I brought in. I wanted to give you the raw data, as I always do," Craig said in a more subdued tone. "I'm sorry if I came across as defensive. It's not like me."

"No, it's not," Dr. Oddlove replied, also in a calmer voice. "Let's let it play out with the root cause team and then we can get a briefing from them later today. We'll call DC this evening."

"Roger that, sir. We'll get through this," Craig said in his normal voice as he exited Dr. Oddlove's office.

"I hope so," Dr. Oddlove replied.

As Craig walked back to his office, he received a page from Claire. He looked at his beeper and said, "Now what?" out loud—loud enough to startle the folks he was passing.

At his office, Claire looked up at him and said, "Your wife called and asked that you call her as soon as you get back."

"Okay, I'll call her now," he replied, rubbing his temples. He felt exhausted.

Craig closed his office door. He knew why she'd called. By now, Anne had received the results of her biopsy. Craig began to pray: *God, please let the results be negative. I can't deal with Anne having cancer. Lord, please.* Then he picked up his phone and called her. She answered on the second ring and Craig could hear the bad news in her voice as soon as she said hello.

"Hey, babe. You got the results?"

"I did," Anne said as she began to cry. "I have cancer, Craig, and it's bad. Can you come home?"

"I'll be right home, sweetheart. I'm leaving now."

Craig picked up his briefcase and walked to Claire's desk. "Anne got a bad report from the doctor, Claire, and I need to go help her deal with it. Please tell no one what I just told you—just tell them I had a family emergency. Cancel my meetings, and I'll call you later in the day."

"Is she okay, Craig? What is it?"

"It's not good. I'll tell you more when I can, but please tell no one of it."

"Got it, sir. Good luck."

As Craig drove home, his mind oscillated between replaying what had already happened at work and imagining what was still to unfold. He brooded over his unusually stressful meeting with Dr. Oddlove and worried about how he'd tell Dick. He wondered how he'd be able to maintain his status as the best general manager in the Weapons Complex and how badly his bonus would be affected. Lastly, a few thoughts about Anne and her diagnosis ran through his mind, briefly contemplating how he'd deal with her, speculating how soon he could return to the office, and hoping Dr. Oddlove wouldn't request the DC briefing while he was still at home.

Once again, I was utterly shocked by his thought process. It was as if he saw Anne's cancer as just another stressful hassle. He wasn't even that worried about her. On the other hand, I was distraught. I loved that humble, delicate, loving woman. She was everything to me. She was my rock during problems and times of crisis. How could Craig not be ripped apart right now? Why wasn't he crying? How could he be more concerned about work?

***

Craig opened the unlocked door to his home, walked in, and put down his briefcase. Their house was in Woodside Plantation, the nicest subdivision in Aiken. Overlooking the eighteenth tee, the huge, stucco colonial was beautiful. Craig had contracted out the landscaping, and it was immaculate. The backyard boasted a luxurious swimming pool and jacuzzi, where Craig and Anne would often go to relax and talk together. But those talks had become less frequent and meaningful over the past year as Craig had grown increasingly distant. Initially, Anne felt hurt, but she tried to convince herself the change was work related and would be short-lived. However, it was becoming harder for her to ignore and excuse Craig's behavior. Things were different somehow. She couldn't put her finger on it, but she knew all was not right.

"Hi there, sweetheart," Craig said as he found Anne standing alone in the kitchen clutching a cup of lukewarm coffee.

"Hi," she said and turned to Craig. As they hugged, she began to cry. "I've got cancer. I've got breast cancer. I'll need a mastectomy; I just know it. I'll never be the same."

"Honey, you don't know that yet; you couldn't. It may be better than it appears. Let's sit down while you tell me everything."

"The doctor was actually the one who called, so I knew it was bad news when I heard his voice. He simply said that the biopsy was positive for cancer. He apologized but stressed there was no need to panic; said he wanted to see me at nine tomorrow morning to discuss a treatment plan. I know I should have asked him more, but I couldn't. I just said I'd be there tomorrow and hung up. I needed to get off the phone before I broke down and started crying."

"I'm sorry, honey. I truly am, but I'm sure everything will work out. It always does. God has been so good to us. There is no way this thing can defeat us."

Thankfully, yet inexplicably, Craig had returned to himself. I was grateful to be back in charge once again. Craig was fighting back tears and finally realizing who had cancer. It was his wife, the woman he loved more than anyone else in the world. The amazing woman who had been the single biggest force in his success. It was Katy's mom. It was Anne. God, it's good to have Craig back, I thought, at least for now.

FIRST PRINCIPLES
Fall Leaves (2013)

It was Sunday and a beautiful April day in Atlanta. Trees were beginning to flower, grass was beginning to green, and the sticky pine pollen was in the air. The heat and humidity hadn't arrived yet, but it wouldn't be long. Taking full advantage of the picture-perfect spring day, Katy was dressed in running shorts and a workout top and planned to drive to the park near her house for a run after a short visit with her dad. She attended the early service at her church, made a quick wardrobe change, then headed to Fall Leaves, arriving just after lunch was served.

Her initial greeting with Craig had gone well as his brain acknowledged her and registered happiness. She even managed a smile from Betty, though the look on her face told Katy she wasn't completely certain who she was. But the vibes were good. Katy was quietly watching them eat when Levi walked up and joined them.

"Hi, Katy," he greeted her as he reached the group.

"Hello, Levi. It's good to see you."

"Hi, Mom. Hi, Craig. How's your day going?"

Betty looked up, this time smiling heartily. She knew it was Levi.

"Hey, son. How are you?"

"Doing fine. Just wanted to see your pretty face."

Craig felt his normal trepidation about Levi, forced a tepid smile, and continued eating.

"Join us, Levi? We're having an exciting time here," Katy said.

Levi laughed. "Why don't we talk while they finish eating, if you've got a little time? Looks like you're dressed for a run."

"Sure, sorry about the outfit." Katy stood and whispered her thanks to Levi for rescuing her from the silence.

The two of them found seats in the waiting area and made small talk about each other's family and the latest on Craig and Betty, who were now inseparable. Betty only went to her room to get clothes. They ate, slept, exercised, played bingo, and took part in all other Fall Leaves activities together. A couple now acting as if they'd been together for thirty years, reverting back to the auto behaviors they were comfortable with during their married lives. The match was perfect.

"It's amazing to see your mom and my dad now. They're always together."

"I know, and while I was very uncomfortable with it at first, I'm getting used to it."

"Me too," said Katy. "I don't think they really understand their relationship, but it has been a true blessing for my dad. He seems so much more content now, and the angry spells rarely happen anymore."

"Same with my mom. She seems happy, and that makes me happy."

"Does your dad ever talk about your mom? Anne was her name, right?"

"Yes, to both. Her name was Anne, and Dad asks about her from time to time, though not as much lately. Usually, he asks when we are in his room and he sees her picture on the table. He asks where she is and if she died. I give him a brief summary of how she died and a few highlights of their life together. He used to cry occasionally, but not lately."

"She died of cancer, right?"

"Yes. It's a sad story on many counts. Although I hadn't fully grasped it, Dad was already slipping into dementia when Mom was diagnosed. She found a lump on her breast that was cancerous. After more diagnostics, it actually turned out to be stage four. Her body fought it for a time, but she passed two years after the diagnosis. I was just starting my law career and still regret not spending more time with her," Katy said as she teared up. "I made a lot of mistakes during that time."

"What do you mean?" Levi gently asked.

"Well, my dad had always been this successful professional. He ran nuclear businesses as a contractor for the federal government. Though I tried, I never really understood what he did, but he was successful and made a good living from it. Anyway, during Mom's illness, Dad was changing. I didn't really know what was going on, or maybe just refused to see it, but I often got upset with him during her illness because he didn't seem worried or caring enough. He wasn't giving Mom the attention she deserved. I just couldn't believe how he was acting during Mom's fight with cancer. Apparently, Dad was also having real problems at work, significant problems. He made some major mistakes."

Katy chewed her lip for a moment, then looked down at the floor.

"I can now admit that for several months I essentially ignored the evidence that Dad might have a form of dementia or something else. He had grown very forgetful and was just acting differently. I should have acknowledged it and taken him in for evaluation. Instead, I remained focused on my career. I didn't help Mom as much as I should have, and I was very angry at Dad. I was mad, and I said mean things to him. I accused him of being a narcissist who didn't love Mom. I couldn't help myself. I was so selfish," Katy said as tears streamed down her cheeks.

"Don't be so hard on yourself, Katy. I totally understand. I was so mad at Mom for being with your dad that I wanted to stop visiting her. I just kept asking myself, how could she?"

They smiled sadly at each other. Levi kept silent for a moment, then decided to change the subject.

"So, I've thought a lot about your opinions on predestination and faith, and your thoughts about why bad things happen. Do you have it in you to listen to my amateur thoughts?"

"Of course," Katy said with a chuckle. "I'd love to hear!"

"Well, I find the faith and predestination arguments to be somewhat convincing, especially with the hedge on predestination. However, I really have a hard time with the belief that tragedies, like dementia, are somewhat insignificant in relationship to eternity. I mean, I get what you're saying, but it's a hard pill to swallow."

"I warned you," Katy said.

"Yes, you did. I need to think more on it and maybe it'll grow on me. My question for today is only related tangentially."

"Nice word," said Katy.

"Thanks," Levi said with a smile. "So, your dad was a fine, upstanding, steadfast Christian all his life, right?"

"Right."

"So, he gets this horrible disease, but it's seen as moot, right?"

"Well, like we discussed, it's not moot to me or him for the here and now, but maybe, and I stress that *maybe*, in light of eternity, it is."

"I know. I was just throwing the 'moot' in there to see if you were listening." Levi grinned.

"Gotcha," Katy said as she nodded.

"Forgive what I'm about to say, Katy. I don't really mean it, but I tend to grossly overstate things for effect. It's just to get my point across. Is that okay?"

"Sure, Levi. I can take it."

Levi paused for a second, then began again: "So, your dad, this fine, upstanding Christian, gets this disease, a disease that was in no way his fault, and suddenly he's a different person. He's now Craig, the bigot; Craig, the masher; Craig, the curser; Craig, the Hun. How does that happen? Where is the old Craig? Is he now possessed? Is he now someone else? Or maybe this is the real Craig?"

Katy watched him, her eyes widening. Levi drew in a short breath and continued.

"So, here's my question. Is this whole thing about soul and mind real, or is there just a brain in there that's misfiring and that's all there really is? If you chose the first one, then why the total change in personality and where is the soul? If you chose the second, he's just a lump of matter that contains this set of wires that are now misfiring and shorting out. His conduct change is simply him losing access to the parts of the brain that filter his behaviors. Memes and such, I think they're called."

"Dude! You're killing me. So now you want to talk about being a dualist or monist? Talk about some heavy stuff!" Katy redid her ponytail. "You've been reading about this, haven't you? The way you phrased your questions makes me think you have. I mean, who uses the term *meme*?"

"I guess I have," Levi said shyly, in stark contrast to his persona. "I've read all sorts of books on dementia. They cover it from a physical, psychological, spiritual, and even metaphysical standpoint, though I'm still not sure what metaphysics is. Heck, I'm not even sure what psychology is and if it's real. But I digress. So, who is Craig now?"

Katy sat quietly pondering the question. "To be perfectly honest, I really don't have a good answer for you, Levi. I've had the same question, though, and I've also read up on it, even about theories relating consciousness to quantum entanglement. I'm just not sure what's going on. I am obviously a dualist; I guess all Christians are. I believe in a soul that will live on into eternity, but how that all works inside my brain and the brain of my dad and your mom is another question. At times, it seems that my dad is back. He seems almost like he always did. Other times, I have no idea who I'm talking to. Then I think, if I'm talking to someone else, where is my dad?

This is where the monists have their best argument, I guess. They'd say that the brain is just malfunctioning, making the person act and speak out of character. In theory, it's similar to how a person acts when drunk. Alcohol affects the brain, which, in turn, affects behavior. Dementia seems no different. It's just shorting out your wiring, so, of course, you'll act differently.

"Where the monist argument falls apart is consciousness itself. They really can't explain why we feel conscious. They believe it's just an illusion that developed over time that was part of preservation of the species. You know, the feeling that you're inside your own head, calling the shots. Kinda like a control room operator in one of the stories my dad would tell me about the nuke plants he worked in. You've got this guy sitting at a control panel pushing buttons and watching screens. That's how I see myself inside my head. I'm sitting at a control panel receiving input from my body and surroundings, like being bitten by a mosquito or hearing a baby crying, then I make the call on what to do about it.

I guess if I had to come up with an answer to your question, Levi, I'd say that with dementia, the guy at the control panel is having a much harder time controlling the nuke plant because the dementia is causing the panels to short out, and maybe the plant is just running itself from its software or something like that."

Katy stretched her legs out in front of her, then crossed them at the ankles under her seat. "So, I guess what I'm saying is that sometimes my dad's soul is in charge and sometimes his brain is running itself. Honestly, I really can't be certain, but it's the best I can do on short notice."

Levi sat back and said nothing for a minute. Finally, he said, "Thanks, Katy. I really hope I didn't offend you with the things I used in my example. I can be pretty blunt."

"No problem at all. I know where your heart is, Levi. I really think God is talking to you now. I think you're working out your faith and that you'll soon be a believer like me. I'm praying for you. So is Thomas, by the way."

Levi smiled and said, "Maybe, but in the meantime, I've got even more to think about."

"Please keep thinking, but remember that in the end, it's all about faith," Katy said.

As they finished, Katy noticed that Thomas was sitting with Craig and Betty. She and Levi joined them as they finished eating lunch.

"Hey, Katy. Hey, Levi. I didn't see y'all."

"We were in the waiting area over there. Levi was asking me all kinds of questions about the duality of man. You know, questions about how dementia works, why personalities change, fundamentals."

"Yikes!" said Thomas. "Those are fathomless questions."

Normally, they would never talk about dementia or memory around their parents for fear of upsetting them. However, it wasn't a hard-and-fast rule, and at times like this, they just did.

"Wish I'd seen you both earlier so I could have joined you. Probably best, though, if we save these topics for another time and place," Thomas said as he cast a protective and pointed glance at Craig and Betty.

"Right," said Levi. "To be continued."

At this, I wanted to scream. Keep going, I thought, I'm in here, and I'm losing control. Oh, how I wish I could tell them what was happening, but I couldn't.

DETONATION
Tritium (2005)

As Craig was at home comforting Anne, Dr. Oddlove was on the phone with DC.

"I'm afraid we are going to require a Readiness Review prior to restart," NA-1 said to Dr. Oddlove. "You and Craig probably don't think one is warranted, but we do. We can talk about the level of review, but a review will be required."

Dr. Oddlove sighed heavily. He figured this was coming. "Okay, sir. I get it. I won't try and push back."

NA-1 was surprised by this. "Really?" he asked. "I had expected a small skirmish."

"Sorry to disappoint you, sir, but I actually agree with your decision."

"Why is that?" NA-1 asked.

"I think our contractor is slipping a bit. The Tritium facilities are still the best-run facilities in the complex, but I have been a bit concerned of late."

"Really? Why? Give me specifics."

"Well, first, I think they've been too concerned with efficiency. Don't get me wrong; we always want to be good stewards of the taxpayers' money, but without inappropriate risk. You know, risk and reward. I just feel that some of the things they have done lately have been too risky for the potential reward."

"For instance?" NA-1 pushed.

"The best example I can think of offhand is the review they performed prior to installing the new upgrade in our facility control system. They did it quickly in spite of warnings we gave them. The software also contained a learning function for some sections that used algorithms to evaluate data it collected and made recommendations to improve efficiency. An AI function of sorts. We were leery, but they installed it. Maybe we should have stopped them."

"Why are you so concerned about this one example?" NA-1 asked. "It doesn't sound all that egregious to me."

"Well, sir, my facility rep thinks this upgrade may have been a causal factor or maybe even the root cause of the glove box release."

"You're kidding. How so?"

"We aren't sure yet, but we'll know within a few days."

"Okay," said NA-1. "I'll get started on a Readiness Review charter and select the team. I'll call you tomorrow with more details so we can get started and work to get this facility back up and running as soon as possible."

As he wrapped up the conversation, Dr. Oddlove thought about how unusual this call had been. Typically, he was one of the strongest advocates for Craig and the contractor team, and he would have pushed back on the review with all his might. But something had changed, starting with the discussion he and Craig had earlier. Dr. Oddlove was confounded by Craig's defensive disposition. He also felt that Craig was trying to point fingers at him and DOE. He'd never had these thoughts about Craig before, but he did now.

Dr. Oddlove pressed the button to end his call with NA-1 but kept the receiver in his hand. He pushed the autodial button for Craig's line and Claire answered after the first ring.

"This is Dr. Oddlove. May I speak to Craig, please?"

"Hello, sir. I'm sorry but Craig had to go home to take care of some important personal business."

"When will he be back?"

"I'm not sure, sir. Shall I page him?"

"Yes. I need him to call me as quickly as possible."

Claire was torn. She knew that Craig never left the office in the middle of the day. Whatever was happening had to be serious. However, she had crystal clear directions from Craig that she was to page him at any hour of the day or night if the customer needed him. She paged him.

As Craig and Anne sat quietly holding hands on the sofa, he saw that Claire was paging him and knew she wouldn't have done so if it wasn't important.

"I need to call the office, Anne. I'm sorry."

"That's fine, honey. Go ahead. There's nothing we can do here anyway but wait and pray. Go on back whenever you need to. I'll be fine."

Anne was a saint, having always allowed Craig to make his job his top priority. She knew how much he loved Katy and her, but she also recognized how important his career was to him and worked hard to make certain he was not distracted by things at home.

Craig called Claire from their landline. "What is it, Claire? Something happen?"

"No, sir. It's just that Dr. Oddlove asked me to page you."

"Did you tell him I was offsite?"

"I did, but he still wanted you paged."

Craig felt a suffocating fog of concern surround him. Dr. Oddlove knew he had left the facility and was probably assuming Craig was taking the whole matter too lightly.

"Please call him. Tell him I'm on my way back and that I'll be in his office in about an hour. Page me if that doesn't work."

"Yes, sir. I'm sorry I had to disturb you. Is Anne okay?"

"Yes, Claire, and thanks for asking. And you did the right thing in paging me. See you in a bit."

***

Walking into Dr. Oddlove's office, Craig could feel the tension in the air, see it on Dr. Oddlove's face, and hear it in his voice.

"Please sit down, Craig." He didn't offer a cordial greeting. He also didn't show concern or inquire about the personal business that had called Craig away from the facility. "NA-1 called while you were out. He's requiring a Readiness Review prior to restart. There is no dissuading him, and he's already working on the charter and team."

"You're kidding!" Craig blurted as his face turned red and his muscles tensed. "That's ridiculous. We don't need a damn review."

"Need it or not, it's coming, and you better get your troops ready to pass it quickly."

"If there's a review, we won't be able to start loading again until we pass it. Those things can take weeks, or even months. Did you tell them it's totally not necessary? There is no way we need a Readiness Review, sir, no way."

"Craig, stop. It's going to happen. What's going on with you? Do I need to send you a letter? I expect you to accept it, put together a plan to limit the size and duration of the review, and get on with it."

"You are aware that if DOE mandates this review, we will miss shipments? We have a full month's maintenance that must be done prior to restart as well. We might be able to do some prior to and during the review, but those review guys tend to want the facility in total shutdown. Your prophesy of missing a shipment will come true."

"So, now you're threatening me with missed shipments if the review is required, Craig? You're threatening me?"

"No, sir. We're in this together—I just want you to know what I know."

"I've heard that line before. Just go back and get your folks ready for the review. NA-1 should have a draft of the specifics to be reviewed in the morning. That is all."

Craig had never had a conversation with Dr. Oddlove like this one. Not even close. They were friends who trusted each other, or at least they used to be. Now their relationship was strained and full of tension and mistrust, the kind that some of the other contractors had, the kind he had always worked so hard to avoid.

Confused, Craig walked back to his office with his head down. His world was coming apart. The worst was actually happening. The event, his customer relationship, and, of course, Anne's diagnosis.

On his desk was a note to call Mary, the corporate assist team lead. He sat down and dialed her number.

"Hello, this is Mary."

"Hi, Mary. This is Craig. What's up?"

"I just wanted to give you a report on my conversation with Stacy and Tom and where the root cause team currently stands."

"Please do."

"Well, let me start with Stacy and Tom. As you would guess, Stacy took it hard, but she took it. She is very worried about her facilities, the maintenance backlog, and, of course, shipments. She's been so focused on facility recovery that she is here nearly 24/7. She needs a break, but the event room has been recovered and gas purification is working as designed. She feels normal operations and maintenance can resume later this week, and she's got a plan for shipment recovery, but that will take some coordination with the Department of Defense. She thinks we can avoid the missed shipment scenario. However, her assumption does not include a true software fix to the AI loading issue. We can put a patch on it to keep it from generating suggestions, but a total fix will take six to ten weeks just to design, and then there's the outage needed to install it."

"How did Tom take the news?"

"He's still in denial and believes the only mistake made was by the operator. I tried to explain nicely that his folks should have asked for help when they didn't understand the reports, but I don't think I got through."

"Their reactions are exactly what I expected," said Craig. "How about the root cause team?"

"They have become energized by our revelation and are working feverishly to complete their report, but I'm afraid it will be pretty much the same as the briefing I gave you."

"That's to be expected, Mary. You and your team have done a great job. Have you given a status update to Dick or Fran back in DC?"

"I do keep Fran in the loop," Mary replied, "but so far, I've simply said that we found a software glitch that may have caused the release. I don't think she understands the gravity of it yet. I have intentionally downplayed it for you, Craig. I figured that you'd want to tell Dick yourself and spin it however you think best."

"Thanks, Mary. It's nice to have someone with both your technical acumen as well as your political savvy. I truly appreciate it. You and your team are free to go back whenever you feel comfortable turning it over to engineering and the root cause team."

"It's been our pleasure. I will get with Tom and the root cause team to begin our exodus. We will likely be gone by the end of the week."

After hanging up, Craig asked Claire to page Tom and Stacy and have them come to his office. Then he stared once again at the photo on his wall of a ground detonation at the Nevada Test Site, taken in the early 1960s at the end of atmospheric testing. The words at the bottom: "Tritium, Keeping the Peace." The picture had been a gift from HQ for a series of accomplishments several years ago, but it all seemed meaningless to Craig at the moment. The mushroom cloud was now his life.

Claire walked in and reported that Tom and Stacy would be up to see him in fifteen minutes, but Craig's mind was blank. He could not focus and suddenly felt no concern for the various problems in his life. All his worries instantly left him.

Was God bringing him peace, I thought? No such luck. He was once again entranced with Claire, staring and smiling at her.

"Come on in, Claire," he said. "There's a lot going on right now, but at least I've got you to help me through it."

Oh no, I thought. Evil Craig is back.

"Um, thank you, sir," Claire replied, a little confused. Craig had never said anything like that to her before.

"If I weren't married, I'd ask you to massage my shoulders. I'm so tense."

Claire was floored, offended, and a bit frightened. Who was this? Wasn't his wife facing some sort of adversity at home? *I've got to get out of here*, she thought.

She looked down at the floor and told Craig she'd send Tom and Stacy in when they arrived.

Unfazed by her reply, Craig kept staring at her as she left.

In what seemed like a mere thirty seconds, Tom and Stacy were at his door.

"Come in. Have a seat. Well, it looks like we now know what happened. It's just a matter of time until the root cause team issues their report. It won't be pretty for us."

Stacy had been making only occasional eye contact with Craig as he spoke, but once he finished she looked him in the eye and said, "Exactly, sir. Unfortunately, that's how I see it too. There is plenty of blame to go around, including operations. We should have stopped loading operations when the new window came up, but we didn't. However, DOE and the root cause team will go easy on operations because they'll believe the operator was set up. I'd take the whole blame if I could, sir. It would be so much easier just to blame operations, which would get us up and running again much quicker, but it won't happen.

"My concern now, sir," Stacy continued, "is that we will be required to do a Readiness Review prior to restart. We've heard rumblings from Hidebound that HQ may mandate one."

"Well, he's right," Craig said. "I just got off the phone with Dr. Oddlove, and it's coming. HQ will have the criteria outline for us soon. As we speak, they are in the process of selecting a team to conduct it."

"Oh no," she said, shaking her head. "I was afraid of that. Those things can take weeks or months and won't even get started for a week or so. I had a plan to work a 24/7 maintenance outage, beginning this weekend, and then resume operations. If the review occurs, we will not be able to meet shipments. No way."

At this, Tom could keep quiet no longer. He had been patiently listening to Stacy, but now it was his turn.

"I don't think I agree that the software caused this, Craig. I think that the software did just what it was supposed to, and we knew exactly what it might do. We did understand those reports and were addressing them. I am offended by your representation otherwise. Operations should have caught the new window and stopped, so engineering could have evaluated it. But they didn't. I will rebut anything the root cause team says to the contrary."

This ignited Craig.

"Shut the f—k up, you narrow-minded asshole! Just shut up! I ought to fire your dumb ass right now, and I will if you say another word!"

Tom's face turned crimson, his Alabama school colors. He was in shock, visibly shaking, and tearing up. He stood to his feet, his legs wobbly, and said, "I don't have to take that kind of profane, verbal abuse. I'm outta here." He stormed out of the office.

Stacy was floored as well and had no idea what to say. This was not the boss she so respected.

"This isn't you, sir," she stammered. "When did you start cursing at your staff? I'm worried about you, Craig. You need to go home and put things in perspective."

The silence between them lasted nearly a minute.

Finally, Stacy stood up and said, "I'm going back down into the facility. I'll get our team together and come up with a plan that somehow integrates the Readiness Review with the maintenance outage. Please send me the HQ criteria when you get it. I will look it over for you and make suggestions to keep it as narrow as possible so maybe we can do the full outage in parallel. Maybe, just maybe, this will work out. But, sir, we need you to get back to your calm, strategic self, or we're not gonna make it. We need you."

Stacy left Craig's office and headed down to the facility. Tom, however, had gone directly to the director of human resources. He'd already explained what happened in Craig's office, was filing a formal complaint, and contemplating whistle-blower status.

After Stacy left, Craig called his boss.

"Hey, Dick; it's Craig. Let me start by thanking you and Fran for the use of Mary and her folks. They were wonderful and got right to the issue. I don't think they've left the facility since they got here. They're almost finished now, though, and should be headed back your way in a day or two. The customer appreciated it very much as well."

It was out of character for Craig to be disingenuous and flippantly upbeat about such a serious matter. I didn't know if Craig was doing so intentionally, hoping the situation would work out better than expected, or if he simply was no longer concerned about the issue. I just couldn't tell.

"What did they come up with? Fran called yesterday and said Mary thought she'd found the issue but was somewhat foggy on the actual cause. So, where are we, Craig?" his boss asked.

"Um, looks like operator error," Craig said. "This software apparently worked just as expected and gave operations some options they took but shouldn't have. I think it'll all work out fine. The event room is now fully recovered, and we are working out the necessary maintenance details before we restart. That shouldn't be a big deal, though. Stacy is working with DOD to use some schedule float, so we won't have to miss any shipments. Should be a happy ending."

Dick was silent for a moment. "Craig, some of our folks were in Forestall yesterday, and there was a lot of talk about the mess that Tritium is in. It wasn't good talk. They heard reports of DC requiring a Readiness Review. Have you heard that? Are you telling me everything, because this seems like a big deal?"

"No, I haven't heard that, Dick," Craig lied. "They wouldn't require that for operator error."

"I hope you're right, but you know DOE never wants to blame an operator. It's always a systematic or culture issue with them. I think you better take off your rose-colored glasses."

"Let me see what else I can find out, Dick. I'll get back to you as soon as I know more, but I wouldn't worry. This is Tritium we're talking about here."

Craig had left his door open and was speaking loudly. Claire was in shock as she heard him lie to Dick. Furthermore, he had just done what he had cussed out Tom for doing. He was making excuses and being a hypocrite. She couldn't reconcile this side of her boss with the side she was accustomed to. He never lied, seldom raised his voice, never used profanity, and certainly never made suggestive comments to her.

***

The next morning, Craig arrived early at the office. He and Anne had spent the night talking about her cancer. Neither of them had slept well. In a few hours, she was going back for more testing. Craig contemplated what he would do if Anne's diagnosis was really serious. He tried to pray, but it seemed like he was just going through the motions. His mind wandered back to the problems at Tritium, but even those seemed meaningless. Focusing on either issue and developing a plan forward was impossible. Craig was known for his ability to assess problems and come up with solutions, but not now. He didn't feel right, didn't feel like himself. He knew something was off.

So did I. I was praying nonstop but couldn't get through to Craig, except for short periods of time. Even then, whatever I accomplished during those moments was short-lived. As soon as I lost contact with Craig, the progress I'd made was lost as well.

Craig checked his email and opened a new one from Dr. Oddlove, titled "Readiness Criteria." It read:

Craig,

Attached is the criteria HQ sent me last night for the ORR. Please review it and respond with feedback early this morning. I'm not sure it can be changed, but I'd still like your input. Also attached is a list of team members for the review. I don't want your input on that, as it is already finalized. The review can start no earlier than next weekend, but it can be pushed out if you need more time. However, I wouldn't delay unless you absolutely must

because the review is more comprehensive than I expected
and will likely take two weeks or more to complete.

Opening the first attachment and looking over the criteria, Craig noted it was extensive and included a full review of most engineering practices, operations procedures, and maintenance backlog. Fear and dread began to build in the pit of his stomach. Based on the criteria, the review would take more than a month, and he doubted HQ would allow meaningful maintenance to be performed during that time.

Next, he opened the list of review team participants. It was a who's who of "gotcha guys," as Craig called them. Guys intent on showing how smart they were. Guys who would delight in picking apart Tritium. It would be a dream come true for them, but a nightmare for Craig.

He forwarded the email to Stacy, asked her to look it over, and then come to his office to discuss it. As Craig finished, he noticed that Claire was not at her desk and went to investigate. No sign of her. He returned to his desk to finish his emails.

About half an hour later, Claire arrived. After putting her purse and lunch on her desk, she walked into Craig's doorway. "Sorry I'm late, Craig. I had to make a stop this morning."

"No problem. I'm expecting Stacy. Please send her in when she arrives."

The stop Claire had made was to the HR department for an appointment she'd requested the day before. She'd spent a painful hour detailing her concerns about Craig's continued sexual harassment, of his verbal abuse to Tom, and of the lies he told his boss about the review. She'd broken down and cried while covering it all and was now emotionally drained and second-guessing her actions. Feeling like a traitor, she sat at her desk and tried to focus on the day ahead, but what she really wanted to do was go to her car and cry. Mustering her strength, she worked to keep it together, and when Stacy arrived, she sent her into Craig's office with a wave.

Stacy rushed in, talking nervously. "I've reviewed the criteria, sir, and it's terrible. They want to look at essentially all aspects of engineering. I mean, not just the software upgrade or even the facility control system. They want to look at virtually all engineering practices. It's as if they think engineering has a complacency problem. I know where they're going. And they want to look at operations in the same light. Given these criteria, sir, we also won't be able to do much maintenance. I'm very worried."

"Good morning, Stacy. Please, sit down."

Stacy blew out a breath as she sat, murmured good morning, and asked him how he was feeling.

"I'm fine, Stacy. Why do you ask?"

"Well, after yesterday, I was worried about you. I've never seen you act or talk like that."

"Like what?" Craig asked sincerely.

"Um, you cussed out Tom, for one."

Craig had only a vague recollection of the meeting the day before. It was all a fog.

"I did? Well, I guess it was all the stress. I will apologize to him. I'm planning on asking Dr. Oddlove to narrow the scope somewhat and see about focusing on the facility software and the control system in general, which would include how operations runs it. That should allow us to get through it in a week. If they do what they've suggested, God knows where they'll go."

"I think that's a good idea, sir. Would you like me to draft something for you to send?"

"No, I've got it."

"Okay, moving to another awful issue," Stacy said. "I read a draft report from the root cause team today. It's another stinker. The DOE facility reps on the team are making it to be about as bad as it could be. We mitigated it to some extent, but it's still devastating."

Craig was listening but his mind was jumping from topic to topic, catching the gist of what Stacy was saying but also thinking of Anne, of Claire, and of playing baseball as a kid.

"Okay," he said. "I'll send off an email to Dr. Oddlove, but I think we are pretty well-cooked here."

Stacy looked mystified. She had expected words of wisdom, encouragement, a strategy, anything. But what she got was a puzzled look from her leader that was totally out of context for the gravity of the situation.

"Okay," she mumbled as she stood up. "Let me know what I can do to help." She walked through the door and back to the facility.

Craig drafted a short, halfhearted email asking Dr. Oddlove to narrow the focus of the review. Shortly after pressing the send button, his phone began to ring. It was Dr. Oddlove.

"I got your email," he began with no small talk. "You're asking me to limit the scope but provide no basis for your request? What's the matter with you? You know I need some meat or they will summarily deny it, Craig. This isn't your first rodeo; you know all this. Do you want to try and limit it or not? If you do, I'll need a strong basis."

"I think our basis is that we are Tritium. I mean, we are the best-run facility in the complex and HQ knows that. That should be enough."

"You've got to be kidding," Dr. Oddlove snapped back. "You're delusional, Craig. If that's your answer, I will just send back a 'good-to-go-as-is' to HQ. I'm not going to ruin my reputation on this. I'm very disappointed in my contractor. Goodbye."

Craig hung up the receiver and leaned back in his chair, annoyed but not angry. In fact, he seemed to be at peace.

Though he somehow felt he should be, he wasn't worried either. I was.

***

At 5:30 p.m., Craig was finishing up reviewing and signing off on a stack of papers on his desk when Claire appeared in his doorway. She had made virtually no contact with him throughout the day, but he hadn't noticed.

"Dick is on the phone for you, Craig."

"Thanks, Claire."

"Hello, Dick. How's it going?" Craig asked as he pushed the speaker button on his phone.

"Not good, Craig. Not good at all. Am I on speaker?"

"Yes," Craig said as he picked up his receiver, "but not now. I picked up."

"You lied to me, Craig, and I want to know why."

"What do you mean, Dick? I don't lie."

"You never have before and that's what makes this call so hard. I've put all the pieces together. I now know that there will be a Readiness Review required before you can restart Tritium. I now know that it's a fairly broad review and that the team members conducting it are SOBs. I now know that you did not respond well to your customer about the review, and to him, you seem to be out to lunch. My God, Craig! You're riding one of your warheads toward ground zero. This is so not like you.

Given your past performance, I could put up with the whole thing, but lying to me is unforgivable. I'm on your side, Craig, and you put me in a very bad position, put me in a very bad light with HQ. I got a personal call from NA-1 today, and it wasn't pretty. He was screaming at me for half an hour. I just took it, said I was sorry, and told him I'd get back to him in the morning. It appears his rage was largely due to a call he'd received from Dr. Oddlove. You've totally ticked him off, and he is no longer defending you. In fact, he's talking replacement. Replacement, Craig. Did you hear me?"

"I did, Dick. I don't know what to say. I heard about the review today as well. This whole thing has caught me off guard."

"Off guard? You're asleep, Craig. Wake up! This is bad. NA-1 says he is already in contact with DOD telling them of your woes. They are essentially admitting that shipments will be missed. Do you know what that means? The expense of that is immense. They will kill us in award fee space, not to mention the dents to our reputation."

Craig had gone completely silent. After a short pause, Dick said, "Are you there, Craig?"

"Yes, sir. I was just thinking."

"Well, pause on your thinking, and let's talk about another potential big problem, as if the doomsday I just described wasn't enough. Earlier today, Fran told me your HR manager called her. It appears you now have several personnel complaints filed against you. You, Craig. Of course, I can't go into detail, but I can tell you that several folks in your facility are not happy with your recent behavior. One complaint is particularly serious. You need to assess how you're acting right now, Craig. I tell you this in confidence, as a friend. I shouldn't have given you this heads-up, but felt I had to."

"I can't imagine employee complaints about me, Dick. What are they about?"

"Craig, you know I can't discuss them. They have to take their own due course, but they aren't good."

Claire could hear most of what Craig was saying and felt like she would throw up. She sat quietly in the terror of the moment. What had she done?

GOOD FROM BAD
Fall Leaves (2014)

For two years, Craig and Betty were inseparable, acting as if they'd been husband and wife for forty years. Having grown accustomed to the relationship, the caregivers at Fall Leaves treated them like an old married couple.

However, Craig was slipping fast, much faster than Betty. Physical therapy, provided by the facility twice a week, did little to help, so he used a walker or wheelchair most of the time. Dementia had narrowed his vision and drastically reduced his muscle coordination, which had caused him to fall routinely. Protests that he needed no damn walker or wheelchair were now fewer and farther between. His mind seemed to have entered a more mellow place.

Betty was as much a caregiver as any of the Fall Leaves employees, except for Thomas. She was like a soft and meek cornerback in man coverage on Craig. She helped him into bed each night and out of bed each morning, and she helped him dress, eat, and go to the bathroom. She even showered with him. And while she really didn't seem to be madly in love with Craig or act in an overtly loving way toward him, her actions spoke love.

Craig seemed to enjoy her company as well, though when Katy had him alone and asked about Betty, his usual response was, "Who?" If Katy persisted, he would often deny even knowing Betty, much less sleeping with her. Katy couldn't be sure if his disavowal was born out of respect for Anne or of shame, or perhaps he truly didn't remember her at times. That was the part that Katy never got accustomed to. She could never be quite sure who she was talking to. Was it her dad, whom she knew so well, or was it someone else, a stranger? Only rarely now did she catch glimpses of her dad, and they were fleeting moments spread out over weeks. Whenever they came and however long they lasted, Katy still loved those minutes and was grateful for them.

During these infrequent moments, I was able to re-engage. My main goal was to show Katy that I was still alive and let her know how much I loved her. I would prompt Craig to say something sweet. Those were moments I cherished too. I saw how much Katy struggled with all of it. Once, she asked Thomas who I was. Where was her dad? She tried not to let me hear those conversations, but sometimes I could.

"I know my dad, Thomas, and when he's here, I love it. But it happens so seldom now. So, let me ask you. Where does Dad go when this other Craig takes over? Is he still here, or has he gone on to heaven? You know my beliefs on all this, but honestly, I remain confused. Am I now simply talking to his brain, not his soul? Do you know what I mean?"

"I do, Katy. I wonder about it as well. Going back to the conversation you had with Levi, I do believe in the soul and the mind. I know they're different yet joined somehow. Fully understanding it all doesn't seem possible, so I just leave it in God's hands. I also enjoy those moments with your dad when he's back with us. He is a good man. And notice, I said 'is,' not 'was.' He's still with us, Katy, although his mind is dying. So, let's enjoy the times he's back, and let God deal with the rest."

I loved Thomas. He could console Katy like no one else. He summarized his thoughts in ways that were so easy to understand and always offered humble wisdom and practical suggestions. None of this was lost on Katy or me.

Katy sighed and nodded, appreciating Thomas's discernment and insight.

After all these years, Thomas still enjoyed his job at Fall Leaves and particularly loved it when people came to him for advice and comfort. He spent hours and hours with Katy and Levi and loved them both. He continued to witness to Levi after that first theological discussion and prayed daily for him.

While Levi had not accepted Christ, he was earnestly contemplating it. He had always been very skeptical of religions but now felt different, a sort of draw toward it. Perhaps it was his conversations with Katy about faith or because he now could accept and even be happy about his mother's new companion, or maybe it was because he had two new faithful friends.

But more likely it was a recent conversation with Thomas. He had asked Thomas about Christianity in a very general way and its relevance to a Jewish friend of his. Thomas explained how Jesus Christ, who himself was a Jew, had come from God, died for our sins, and risen, and that we are now under a period of Grace, no longer the Jewish law, and He was waiting for Levi to accept Him.

But Levi had drawn back in defense and asked Thomas if he was trying to make points with his God. Thomas simply responded in a calm tone that "this isn't football, Levi, and I'm not trying to score. I offer this to you only for you, not me. I offer it because I love you, Levi, and I want you to know Him." I think it was that, the realization of Thomas offering Christianity out of love, not some other motivation, that truly made Levi think.

Shortly after lunch one Monday afternoon, Craig and Betty were sitting at their table in the dining area, staring at the TV on the wall. Both were oblivious to it and most everything else around them.

"You want to go back to our room?" Betty asked.

Craig paused while the question bounced around in his head.

"Okay," he replied.

"Let me come around with your wheelchair."

"I don't need a wheelchair," Craig slurred. His voice had changed dramatically over the past year. Now he spoke in a near-whisper and often started and ended sentences in mid-thought. Rejection of the wheelchair was more of a reflexive response than a cognitive one. Instinctively, he placed his hands on the arms of the chair and began to rock back and forth, triggering a reaction in Betty. She had seen this before and knew it could be trouble, though she wasn't exactly certain why.

Craig's pendulum-like motion hit full stride. As his upper body moved forward on his last rock, he pushed down and stood, unsteady and wobbly. He grasped the chair just in time. He then tried to step forward with his right foot, but it got caught on the chair leg, causing him to fall forward and face-plant onto the tile floor of the cafeteria. The next thing he remembered was the hollow, steel-like feeling he had as a child when he fell off the jungle gym in grade school. Facedown, he lay silently.

Betty shrieked, "Oh my God! He fell! He fell! Someone help him!"

She shuffled as quickly as she could and kneeled beside Craig, who was conscious, but just barely. He rolled onto his side and blood oozed from the open wound on his forehead.

He looked up at Betty and asked, "What happened?"

"You fell, Craig. You fell and you're bleeding too."

The compliance-based caregiver knew just what to do. She called 911 first and then went over to Craig to evaluate the situation. Residents taking tumbles were common occurrences at Fall Leaves. However, per company policy, blood and head trauma required a call for an ambulance. The staff moved the furniture from around Craig, put a pillow under his head, and waited for paramedics. In less than ten minutes, they arrived and rushed in to treat him. They applied a bandage to the huge gash on his forehead, placed him on the stretcher, and rolled him outside.

Thomas had left the facility to run an errand on his lunch break and returned just in time to see them loading Craig into the ambulance.

Alarmed, he asked, "What happened?"

"Just a fall," the paramedic replied, "but he has a doozy of a head injury. We're taking him in for observation. The hospital will be in touch, as usual."

Thomas took Craig's hand as he was hoisted into the ambulance.

"You okay, Mr. Craig?"

"I guess," Craig replied softly. "Where are they taking me?"

"To the hospital. You've fallen again, and this time you bumped your head."

"I did?"

"Yes, you did. I'll call Katy and let her know."

Craig said nothing else as they closed the door of the ambulance.

Thomas returned to the second floor and walked briskly to the nurses' station.

"Have you called Mr. Craig's daughter?" he asked.

"Yes, of course, Thomas. She's en route to the hospital."

Thomas wished he could be there to meet Katy, but he couldn't leave the facility. Praying silently for both Craig and Katy, he walked over to Betty, who was still in the lunch room. She looked lost. Unable to remember exactly what had just happened, she was sad nonetheless.

"You all right, Miss Betty?" She said nothing as she looked up at Thomas. "Mr. Craig fell. Do you remember?"

"Yes," she whispered with uncertainty in her voice.

"Don't worry, Miss Betty. He will be just fine and will probably be back here in time for dinner. Let's go to the TV room now; they're playing a movie."

* * *

Having informed her assistant about Craig's fall, Katy rushed from her office. The scenario had become familiar. She knew the drill and also that so far, her dad had been fortunate—no broken bones or severe injuries. As she drove, she thought about the one just over a month ago. He'd fallen backward and hit his head, requiring five stitches. A few days later, she had stopped Craig as he tried to comb the stitches out. He thought he had gum in his hair and wanted it gone.

At the ER, she asked for directions to her father and quickly found his bed. A young nurse was trying to calm an agitated Craig and clean his wound.

"Why am I here? What are you doing?" he asked the nurse.

"I need you to be still, sir. You have a cut on your forehead from your fall."

"What fall? I don't want to be here. Where am I?"

Katy arrived just in time. "Hi, Dad. You getting into trouble again?" she said in a happy voice.

Craig looked up at her in complete confusion and made no reply as she calmly introduced herself to the nurse.

"Can I speak to you privately for just a second?" Katy asked the nurse.

"I guess so," she replied, and they stepped away and pulled the curtain around the bed.

"I'm sure you know this already, but my dad has dementia. He's not going to be much help to you in evaluating the accident. His short-term memory is only good for a minute or two. He fell at Fall Leaves, which has become fairly common for him. I hate it, but there seems to be no way of stopping it. No matter how much attention he gets, as soon as he gets the chance, he tries to walk and ends up falling."

"I know the scenario well, ma'am. Thanks for the heads-up. Can you help keep him calm while I work on his cut?"

"Sure," Katy agreed as they opened the curtain. "Hey, Dad. How're you doing?"

"Not good. Where am I? Why am I here?"

"You're just in for a checkup, Dad. I know you're in great shape, but you still need that annual exam."

"Oh," said Craig. "Will it take long?"

"No, Dad. We should be out in no time." Katy kept talking while the nurse worked quickly and efficiently to clean and evaluate his wound.

"Someone will be here in a few minutes to take him for an X-ray. After that, the doctor will see him."

As the nurse left, Katy attempted to make small talk with Craig, but he was fairly unresponsive. He just stared into space; the meds he'd been given right before he fell were calming him. Soon, the orderlies came in and rolled him out for the X-ray.

Sitting in the chair next to where Craig's bed had been, Katy called her assistant to let her know what was happening and that she wouldn't be back for the rest of the day. She was immersed in her reading and responding to emails when they brought Craig back. A doctor walked in as well.

"Hi. Are you Mr. Smith's daughter?"

"I am," Katy replied.

"Well, your dad has sustained a pretty severe head injury. There is a hematoma. We need to admit him for the night so we can monitor it. I understand he's a resident of Emerald Hall at Fall Leaves; is that correct?"

"Yes, it is."

The doctor continued, "Seems he's been falling with some regularity and has been here four times in the last year. His records show a fall-related head trauma just six weeks ago."

"That's right," said Katy. "The staff can't seem to prevent it."

"I understand, but this one is worse than the others. We'll get him in a room shortly," he said as he left the room.

Craig seemed oblivious to it all.

"Well, Dad," Katy said, "looks like they need more data on you, so you'll be here for a little while longer."

Craig's consciousness began to fire as he looked at Katy. "Are you my sister?"

"No, Dad. I'm your daughter Katy. You know that."

Craig smiled at Katy. "Oh, yes. My beautiful, smart, lawyer daughter. I love you."

***

Just after eight the next morning, Katy returned to the plastic recliner where she'd spent the night next to Craig's bed. She held two coffees and a chocolate-glazed donut.

"Brought us some coffee, Dad, and your favorite donut."

Craig smiled. "Oh boy, I love coffee and donuts in the morning."

"I know, Dad."

As they sat drinking their coffee, Craig was content. He had no idea where he was or why he was there, but he knew he loved drinking coffee with Katy.

"Where are we?" Craig asked as he took a sip of his coffee.

"We're in the hospital. You had a fall and hit your head." Katy thought she'd give him the truth and see how it went.

"I fell?"

"Yes, Dad, but it's not bad."

Well, the attempt at truth didn't last long, she thought to herself. In fact, Craig's head injury wasn't good. While his hematoma hadn't increased, it was big enough to require treatment, at least under normal circumstances. However, given Craig's mental state, his doctors decided he could return to Fall Leaves and come back to the hospital in a week for reevaluation.

"Hello there."

Katy immediately recognized the voice in the doorway as Levi's.

"Hey, Levi! What are you doing here? Is Betty okay?"

"Sure, she is. Well, maybe not. She's been wandering the halls looking for Craig. She's lost without him; has no purpose." He was smiling, but his tone was serious.

"Oh, that's so sad but sweet. Dad took a pretty bad hit to his head, but they're releasing him shortly. I'll have to bring him back in a week for a reevaluation."

"I'm sorry about your fall and injury, Craig."

Craig just turned his head and looked at Levi. The trepidation had never fully left but now wasn't severe.

"I'm drinking coffee," he said.

"I know, Craig. I bet your daughter Katy brought it."

"She did; she's so good to me. She is paying for all this."

"I know. She's a brilliant, successful lawyer who makes a lot of money."

"She sure does," Craig replied.

"Stop it, you two. You're killing me."

Levi and Katy had grown into more than friends. They were comrades, soldiers fighting their dementia wars together and had their fair share of battle stories to prove it.

Later that day, Craig was released and taken by ambulance back to Fall Leaves. Levi and Betty were waiting for Katy and Craig when they returned. The paramedics rolled him to his room and then moved him to his own wheelchair. Betty looked concerned as she stood over Craig, more like a mother concerned about a child than a wife concerned about her husband. Craig just looked up at Betty and smiled, saying nothing. It was a strange family, but a family it was.

UNCONTROLLED RELEASE
Tritium (2005)

It had been a week since Craig's two blowout conversations with Dr. Oddlove and Dick, and he had talked to neither since. It was the eye of a hurricane. He called Dick several times and left messages, but Dick had not returned them. His calls to Dr. Oddlove netted the same result. It seemed odd to Craig, but he just kept working.

The published root cause analysis was terrible, as expected, and a formal notice from DC was issued stating that the Readiness Review would begin in a few days. It mandated that only maintenance and operations evolutions associated with maintaining their safety envelope could be conducted. Tritium was in chaos. There was little to do except prepare for the review. Maintenance mechanics, operators, engineers—all were pretty much idle, though their managers tried in vain to keep them busy with procedure improvements and other shelved projects. A facility full of dedicated employees with nothing to do but gossip and speculate on how bad things were wasn't good for business. In fact, it was disastrous.

Craig had withdrawn into his office, which didn't help. Tritium employees were accustomed to seeing him daily throughout the facilities, in their offices, the halls, workstations, and even the break areas. The rumor that he had "lost it" and would soon be fired continued to spread, whispered by his employees with knowing and scornful expressions. The way they saw it, he was awaiting the inevitable in his command bunker.

The fact was that Craig had withdrawn, but more from confusion and uncertainty than fear of losing his job. He was having trouble making sense of it all.

"Your wife is on the phone for you, sir. Line one."

"Thank you, Claire," he said.

"Hey, Anne. How's my girl? Everything okay?"

The ensuing silence was a dead giveaway. Craig dreaded the silence most. After a few seconds, Anne began to cry.

"The cancer has spread. It's stage four. I'm going to die."

"My God, honey. How do you know that?"

"The doctor called today with the results from Wednesday's test, and I went in to meet with him. I just got back home."

"I didn't know you were getting your results today, honey. Why didn't you tell me?"

"I couldn't. I know what you're going through at work and just figured I'd go alone."

"I'll be right there, sweetheart. Just sit down. I'll be there in half an hour."

Craig stood up and walked to Claire's desk. "I've got a family emergency and have to go home for the rest of the day. Please clear my calendar and tell anyone who calls that I really can't be reached."

"Is everything okay, sir?"

"No, Claire. No, things are not okay, but I can't talk about it now."

When he arrived home, Craig found his wife in the living room. It was an ornate but rarely used room that Anne loved, filled with furniture from her mother, including the white love seat on which she was sitting. It had a matching sofa and two ladder-back chairs that her father made. She was looking at two nicely framed photos on the end table her father also made. One was a picture of her mother and father dressed in their Sunday best, and the other was Katy's high school graduation photo. Craig went to her, sat down, put his arm around her, and pulled her close. Her eyes were dark from crying.

"What exactly did the doctor say?"

She paused, holding back more tears. "Well, he said that the cancer has spread from my breast and is also in my lymph nodes. I have to go for more tests. He said he wouldn't advise me on treatment until those tests are completed. Those could take several days, but he wants me to check into the hospital tomorrow. I'm so scared."

"I can only imagine, honey. I'm so sorry."

Craig's mind was slipping. Thoughts came and went. He tried to focus on Anne's crisis, but it was difficult. I attempted to get him to pray with me, but it was no use. So I prayed alone. I prayed for Anne and for Craig. We were in the worst spot of our lives.

Craig sat quietly holding Anne and staring into space. She turned and looked into Craig's eyes and sensed his confusion. She knew that Craig was somehow different, but she chose denial, refusing to accept that he was changing quickly for the worse.

"Are things at work any better? You've got so much on you, and now this."

How could she be concerned about Craig when she had just received a death sentence? How could she be so strong? I tried to drive Craig's mind back to her, but again my attempts were futile.

"We've still got some trouble, but it'll be okay. The problem is that we have some incompetent people there. The operators are making mistakes, the customer is being ridiculous, and my boss Dick is being a total jerk."

Craig got up and began to pace the floor. Anne could again feel his confusion. He had become increasingly forgetful and uninterested in things he once loved. He was angry often, and profanity peppered his conversations. Other times, he would just sit by himself for hours. She had avoided thinking about it, but now she had no choice. All the stress was driving him to be a person she didn't know.

"I plan to call Katy in a few minutes. I didn't want to stress her until I knew more, but I guess it's time to tell her."

"I guess you're right. She needs to know. Would you like for me to call her?"

"I don't know. Should you, or should I?"

"Let me do it, honey," Craig said. "I'll call her now from the kitchen phone."

Craig went into the kitchen and called Katy's office. Her assistant put him through to Katy.

"Hey, how's my beautiful lawyer daughter today?"

"Oh, hey, Dad. I'm good. What's up? I can only talk for a minute. I have a client I need to meet with and he's here early."

"I won't keep you long, but there's some bad news that your mom and I feel you need to know. Your mom has cancer."

"Oh no! No! What? What kind? When did you find out?"

"Well, we learned just a little while ago that she had breast cancer, but further tests show that it may have spread. We are going to the hospital together tomorrow for more testing."

Katy fell silent on the other end of the call. Then, she whispered, "Why didn't you tell me sooner, Dad? This is terrible."

"Your mom didn't want to give you the bad news until she knew more. She is being so brave, but it has me beside myself. I don't know what to do, Katy. I've got troubles at work too, and between that and now this, I just don't know what to do."

"You don't know what to do? Of course you know what to do. You be with Mom and forget your job. You pray and pray and pray, Dad, just like you taught me. Let me talk to Mom."

"Okay. Anne, honey, Katy wants to speak to you."

Anne had heard the conversation from the other room and was headed to the kitchen. She took the receiver from Craig.

"Hi, Katy."

"Mom, I'm so sorry." She began to weep, which caused Anne to break down and sob as well. Once she'd recovered, Anne summarized what she knew so far and gave Katy the plan for the next day.

Katy told her mom she wanted to come over to be with her, but Anne insisted there was nothing Katy could do at the moment, but suggested that a quiet talk in the morning would be best for everyone.

Craig and Anne went to bed together that night, but Anne didn't sleep. She stared at the vaulted ceiling in their bedroom while Craig slept, alternating between crying and praying.

In the morning, Craig rose early and dressed for work. He was going into the office for a few hours and would then return to take Anne to the hospital around eleven. His plan was to let everyone at the office know that he'd be off for several days to be with Anne. Katy was coming over in a few hours as well. She planned to be there long before Anne went to the hospital.

They sat together at the kitchen table, drinking coffee in near total silence. Anne looked to have aged ten years, and Craig had a childlike expression on his face, as if he had become helpless and was just waiting for someone to rescue him.

As he picked up his briefcase, he leaned over and kissed Anne on the cheek.

"It will all work out, honey. I'll be back in a couple of hours to drive you to the hospital."

"I love you," she said.

NEXT VOICE YOU HEAR   189

"I love you too, honey. I'm so sorry."

It was nearly eight before Craig arrived at his office. His tardiness was unusual, but Claire simply greeted him and returned to her work. As Craig had walked through the building to his office, everyone seemed to stop talking when they saw him coming. Usually, he couldn't go anywhere in the facilities without sincere greetings and numerous conversations. Tritium had gone silent, at least when Craig was there.

Craig sat at his desk and booted up his computer. As he did, he noticed a message to call Dick. *I'll do that later*, he thought. As the screen of emails lit up, he noticed one from late yesterday with "DOD Shipments" in the subject line. It was actually an email Dr. Oddlove had forwarded to him describing the path forward that NA-1 had brokered with DOD regarding the missed shipments. Not good. NA-1 had informed DOD that their reservoirs would not be shipped on time and that the exact timing was indeterminate. His message went on to explain what this meant to the Weapons Complex and that it was a black eye for all of DOE. Both secretaries were informed.

Craig sat back and stared at the screen. He knew this was ruinous but again could not quite link all the problems together, much less come up with a path forward. Over the years he'd honed the skills to handle critical situations, skills he needed now more than ever. But for now, they were gone.

He picked up the message on his desk to call Dick. He hesitated for a moment and then dialed. Dick's assistant answered.

"Oh, Craig, he's expecting your call. He's on the other line right now, but he wants to be interrupted for you. Can you hold?"

"Sure," Craig replied.

"Craig?" Dick asked.

"Hello, sir. What's up?"

"What's up?" Dick repeated. "Well, Craig, I guess you've seen the email from NA-1?"

"I just read it."

"I shouldn't have to tell you this is about as bad as things get. I guess you know that. You are missing shipments. The department now feels as though you have a major cultural problem in both engineering and operations; you have the worst root cause analysis to fix I've ever seen; and your customer has abandoned you. And to top it off, the employee complaints against you are substantial, corroborated, and, quite frankly, terrible.

"Craig, I'm pulling you out of Tritium. You're not being fired, at least not yet, just being pulled back to DC. The customer has insisted on it, and I agree. You were the best we had; for the life of me, I don't know what happened. I will be there tomorrow morning to meet with Dr. Oddlove and you. Fran will be replacing you, at least on a temporary basis. She'll fly down with me tonight. What I'm asking of you is to not tell anyone until tomorrow. This is a courtesy call that you deserve based on your tenure. We have a press release that will be issued first thing in the morning, but until then say nothing. Do you understand, Craig?"

"I heard what you just said, Dick, but I in no way understand. I can't believe you're replacing me. I've done nothing wrong except try and correct some mistakes our engineering and operations folks made. This whole thing about the culture of engineering is bull----, and the same for operations. This whole thing revolves around a mistake made by one operator—one operator, Dick. We've got the best-run program in the Weapons Complex, and you know it."

"I used to believe that. However, now I'm not so sure, not at all. The facts are clear to me, Craig, and I'd hoped you would have taken this better. But all that aside, I'm replacing you, and that's final. You choose how you'll react. If you make this hard, I'll simply fire you. If you act professionally, I'll bring you back to DC and use you here until a few half-lives have passed on this event and I can find you something back in the field. Do you understand, Craig?"

After a long pause, Craig simply said, "I hear you, Dick. I've got some family issues to deal with now as well, so I will be out the rest of the day. I'd planned to be off the next few days, but I will come back to meet you and Fran in the morning."

Dick was astonished at Craig's plan to take time off. Normally, nothing could have pulled him away from the facility during a crisis, but for now Craig being gone was a good thing.

"Okay, Craig. Take whatever time you need. I'll see you in the morning."

Craig sat back in his chair and again stared at the mushroom cloud that had become his life. He tried to think about each of the catastrophes that surrounded him. He felt betrayed and lonely. He tried to read his emails, but the words he read were just that, words. His mind was racing back and forth. Since he wasn't able to focus on any given email, he sat quietly staring at the screen.

As his mind went back to the conversation he'd just had with Dick, he called Claire into his office.

"Claire, can you have a seat, please? I want to go over a few things with you."

Claire was wearing the most conservative outfit she owned, a pair of light gray dress slacks and a blue blouse buttoned to the top. Sitting in her normal seat with her planner, she was a wreck. Feeling afraid and yet somehow heroic, she was certain that Craig didn't know she was the one who had submitted the employee concern, but she feared he soon would.

"How's your family situation, sir?"

"What do you mean?" asked Craig.

Claire was immediately on the defensive.

"Well, you left early yesterday to address a family concern. I was just wondering if everything is okay."

"Oh. Um, I guess so," said Craig, beginning to understand her question. "Anne has to go in for some tests today, and I need to be with her. They're just tests, so everything should be fine. Thanks for asking," he said in his sweetest voice. "You're such a good assistant."

Claire was immediately stricken by the comment, wondering if he was coming on to her again. She couldn't tell and regretted asking him a personal question. From here on out, it would be business and business only.

"Okay, so you'll be leaving soon?"

"Yes, I'm leaving as soon as we're finished and will be off for the rest of the week as well. I am coming in tomorrow morning for a meeting with Dick and Fran."

"Dick and Fran are coming tomorrow?"

"Yes, they're flying in tonight. Work out the details with Dick's assistant today. I'll come in and meet with them and then be gone for the rest of the week."

"Do you need for me to prepare anything or have some of your staff ready?"

"No, I've got this one covered. It should be a quick meeting."

Claire was confused. Dick never came to town just for a short meeting, usually flying in for a board meeting or other event that required great fanfare. Dick always wanted to meet with Dr. Oddlove and usually Craig's staff. *What was this all about?*, she thought. Sensing Craig's calm demeanor, Claire conceded that everything must be in order.

"Yes, sir. I'll be sure everything is coordinated. I'll page you if the customer or Dick calls—is that still okay?"

"I guess," said Craig. "Whatever you feel is best."

***

When Craig arrived at home, Katy's car was in the drive. He was surprised, even though he knew she was coming.

"Hey, Katy, my pretty and aggressive barrister. How're you doing?"

Katy and Anne were sitting at the table, both with somber expressions and puffy eyes that confirmed they'd been crying for quite some time.

"Hey, Dad," Katy said, totally surprised by his obvious chipper tone and disposition.

Craig sat down with them and became silent at Katy's short response.

"You all right, Dad?" she asked. Anne had again told Katy that her father had become forgetful and peculiar during the past six months. Katy had dismissed her mother's concerns, including the time he'd forgotten to make her dinner, as nothing more than job stress and the normal aging process.

"I'm okay, Katy, just some issues at work. I think I may be transferred to DC soon," he said matter-of-factly, sending shock waves through both Anne and Katy.

"What?" Anne asked in disbelief. "When did this happen?"

"Today. Dick called and said that he might move me to DC, you know, to get some corporate experience."

"In the middle of all that's going on here, how could he possibly move you now? Is it because of the problems? Is he removing you because of what's happened?"

"What's happened?" Katy interrupted.

"Well, we had a dumb-dumb operator make a mistake during a loading operation that resulted in some gas getting into a glove box that's built to handle it," Craig said, his voice getting louder. "Everything worked as designed, but somehow they are making the stupid operator into a hero and blaming me and all of Tritium."

Katy and Anne were both at a loss for words. Silence ensued.

Craig's brain fired again. "Plus, they say that some people have filed complaints against me—sexual harassment, I think." Craig had no idea why he admitted that; with no filter to stop him, it just came out.

Anne grasped the table to keep from passing out, reeling as if she'd been hit by a two-by-four. Katy's eyes widened.

"WHAT? Dad? Is it true?"

"No, of course it's not true. They're just out to get me, that's all."

Katy and Anne could not believe what they were hearing. None of what Craig had said, or the way he said it, seemed possible.

Anne began to weep while Katy stared deep into Craig's eyes with the look of an angry lawyer who had just been deceived. Craig looked shocked and hurt by both responses.

A STRANGE PEACE
Fall Leaves (2014)

It had been a month since Craig's fall. Further testing showed a significant hematoma that wasn't increasing, but it wasn't shrinking either. The only treatment option was surgery, which Katy had declined. Craig's condition had worsened, but it wasn't clear if the injury or his rapidly progressing dementia was to blame. Either way, Craig had become even less responsive, mostly sitting in his room or lying in bed with Betty, who was always near him.

Craig had also developed tremors that kept him from being able to eat. The compliance-based staff was supposed to help him but did so halfheartedly, falling back on the compliance excuse again. When they tried to feed him, he refused to eat. Rather than working with him, the staff simply noted his refusal and went about their business. After they left, Betty would try to coax him into eating, and when Thomas was there he would help. Sometimes they were successful, but Craig had dropped to a mere 140 pounds. His hands, the hands that Katy had loved to hold as a child, were now more like those of a skeleton. His brown dotted skin draped over his bones, with blue vessels showing through. He was wasting away, both in mind and body.

***

Katy and Levi were often there at the same times and talked regularly, and they included Thomas whenever he was available. They could only spend short periods with their parents before the silence drove them to the waiting area to converse. It was a good thing. Both enjoyed the conversations and the ability to break the silence without leaving right away.

In large measure, I was simply a bystander. I watched all that was going on but had little effect on Craig. I too had grown accustomed to his and Betty's relationship and had seen nothing but many positives come from it. Katy and Thomas had led Levi toward God; Craig was now calm and peaceful; Betty was happy with her new mission in life; and Levi and Katy felt more confident about caring for their parents. I guess I was happy too, though I felt useless. I shouldn't say I was useless, though, because I prayed for everyone involved, especially Craig, and God was answering my prayers.

It was now almost seven in the evening. Katy had made it for dinner and dessert with Betty and Craig and afterward walked them to their room. She came directly from her office, as they ate early at Fall Leaves. They wanted to feed the residents before sundown syndrome kicked in. And kick in it did. Katy sat in the waiting area hoping to see Thomas, but he was tied up downstairs helping the assisted living staff. She felt good about being there, doing what she knew a loving daughter should, and it felt like perhaps she was making up for having been hard on Craig when he had been removed from his job.

But Katy had reconciled all that, having realized that his dementia was fast moving and had hit him hard. The man she was so hard on was not her father, but someone else, which was difficult for her to digest. She still struggled with it but could now compartmentalize it into a mental bin by itself and leave it there.

"Hi there." Katy looked up to see Olga. "Do you work here?"

"No, I don't, Olga. Why?"

"Well, if you don't work here, how do you know my name?"

"I occasionally eat meals with you and my dad."

"Hogwash. I don't eat meals here, at least not often. I just came for dinner tonight and they won't let me leave. I need to get home. I just live around the corner. Can you get me out of here?"

"Perhaps you should go to the nurses' station and ask them about it," Katy said.

Olga turned abruptly and left.

Katy just smiled as she walked away. It was time to go. Sundown was here. Katy rose and slowly walked to Craig's room. She knocked politely and entered.

"Hey, Dad and Betty. I'm going to leave now."

Craig was lying on the bed, staring at the TV. Betty was in a chair beside the bed doing the same. Craig looked up and stared at Katy.

He hesitated and then asked, "Are you my sister?"

"No, Dad. I'm Katy, your daughter."

Craig smiled as his mind fired.

"Hi, Katy. You look so pretty tonight. This is my daughter," he said to Betty. "She's a lawyer and pays for all of this for me. She's the best daughter any man ever had. I love her so."

A tear ran down Katy's face. "Thank you, Dad. I love you too."

I had been able to prompt Craig as his brain fired after recognizing Katy. I cherished the moment as well.

Katy walked to the bed and kissed her dad on his forehead, just above the scar from his last fall.

"I'll see you in a few days, Dad. I love you."

UNCLEAR NEXUS
Tritium (2005)

It was now 9:00 a.m. and Craig was walking into his office building. He had stayed up with Anne until nearly midnight.

Katy had been with them for the tests yesterday afternoon but went home around six. Much of that time was spent alone with Craig while they waited for Anne's tests to be finished. The hours with her dad had been long and stressful. Katy was distressed about her mom and the tests she was undergoing, but nearly as burdensome was the news about her father. She asked Craig for more details, but he essentially repeated everything he'd said the day before, offering no additional information. Katy was too smart to buy into it. She knew there was much more to the story than Craig was saying and was confused and hurt. Was her dad some sort of predator? Was he actually not the man she loved? Was he somehow having a midlife crisis or perhaps some sort of mental breakdown? It was more than she could handle, so she would do the only thing she could—immerse herself in her own family and career. The effort would be her opiate.

As Craig entered his office, Claire greeted him. "Good morning, sir. Dick and Fran are in your office waiting for you. They've had coffee and have been here about fifteen minutes."

"Thanks," Craig said.

"Good morning, Dick. Hey, Fran. Good to see you both. How was your flight? Can I get you anything?"

"No, thanks," said Dick. "Our flight was fine, Craig. Why don't you have a seat?"

Craig pulled his planner from his briefcase out of habit and sat at his conference table with them. "What's up?"

"What's up is what we discussed yesterday on the phone. We're here to formally remove you from your role as general manager. You will now be a special adviser in DC and report to me. At least, that will be your title for now. Fran is taking over. The news release is being distributed now. It will be distributed throughout the Forestall and on the Hill to your stakeholders. It will run in the local paper today as well. I sent you a draft yesterday afternoon but got no comments from you, so we went with it. In the email, I also asked to meet with your staff after you'd told them, but again hearing no response, I just went with the email. They will all know soon. I'd advise you to meet with them, Craig, and with Dr. Oddlove this morning. It's the right thing to do for them and for Fran as she takes over."

Craig sat back and stared through Dick. It wasn't an angry look, but it was piercing. After an extended pause, Craig opened his planner, though he really didn't know why. He felt like he needed to make notes on the conversation that was transpiring, but he didn't. Instead, he just focused on the blank pages and finally muttered, "So you're ruining my life because of a dumb operator? Nice. Guess I have no choice but to go along with this."

At this, Dick stood up and briskly walked over to Craig's door, which was slightly ajar, and closed it. He remained standing as he addressed Craig's comment.

"I can't believe that's your response to all this, Craig. I just can't. I'm not going to go over all that's happened again because it's obviously wasted on you. You just don't get it. You also don't get that you have several very serious employee concerns filed against you. One is sexual in nature, Craig, and it seems plausible to me and to HR. I'll expect you out of your office this morning. Fran is now in charge. You can stay and meet with your staff and Dr. Oddlove, but after that you can go home and contact my assistant. She has all the logistics on your job and move to DC."

Craig pondered what Dick had just said. He was angry and confused. How could this be happening?

I tried to calm him and keep him from further self-destruction. It was no use; I had no connection.

Craig bolted up.

"I'll just leave now. I need to be with my wife, who is in the hospital this morning having tests to assess how far her cancer has spread."

"Oh no, Craig," said Fran, darting a look of alarm at Dick. "We had no idea."

"We sure didn't," added Dick. "How is she?"

"She's as good as can be expected, given that she has cancer, but that's not your concern. I will call your assistant when I have time."

"Okay," said Dick. "Why don't you take two weeks' vacation starting today to do what you need to with Anne. You can let me know if you need more time once you've got a better handle on Anne's situation. I'm so sorry, Craig—about Anne and about all of this."

"Thank you both," Craig said as he put his planner back into his briefcase and walked out.

As Craig got into his car, it finally hit him. He had been fired. He had never been fired before. As he sat in his car, he began to weep. He wasn't exactly sure why he was crying, but he was. He felt such pain as his mind envisioned his staff being told he had been replaced. He saw the DOE people he had worked so closely with in DC learning of his fate. He thought about the way

Katy had responded. He thought of Anne having to bear this news along with her cancer and how she looked at the kitchen table when he told her.

He was ashamed. I saw the opening and took it. I replayed his daily devotionals, his talks about God with his father, his Sunday school acceptance of Christ, and how his mom and dad had responded joyously. I reminded him of the joy that he felt most mornings as he prayed. I reminded him of his roots. It worked. He began to pray out loud.

"God, I'm so sorry for all I've done wrong. Please, help me; please, help me now. Please, help Anne. God, this is more than I can bear."

But just as quickly as his old nature had returned, it left. As he drove off toward the hospital, his mind again whirled. The little balls of thought bounced aimlessly in the hopper, with Craig unable to catch any with his consciousness.

Shortly after ten, Craig pulled into the hospital parking lot. He stopped by the gift shop and bought a bouquet of roses for Anne. As he approached Anne's room, he heard his wife and daughter weeping.

"Hey, I brought you flowers," Craig said as he put them on the table next to Anne's bed. "What's wrong, girls?"

Katy looked up at Craig through her tears. "It's bad, Dad; it's very bad."

Craig walked to the bed as tears again welled up in his eyes. He bent over and embraced Anne. "I'm so sorry, baby. We'll get through this together. What exactly did the doctor say, Katy?"

"Well, first he wondered why you weren't here, and we told him you'd be here soon. He wants to meet with you one-on-one today. He said that cancer is throughout her whole body and that he needs to discuss treatment with you."

Anne had stopped crying and taken on a steely look of composure. "I'm here too," she said.

"I'm sorry, Mom. I was just telling Dad what the doctor said."

"I never expected it to be this bad," she said, "but it is, and I'll deal with it with God's help. I don't think I want any treatment; whatever will be will be. I don't want to feel like death for whatever time I have left. I'll just let whatever happens happen."

"Oh, Mom, don't say that. There are new treatments that can work. Many stage-four cancer patients live long lives."

"Not ones who have it in virtually every organ. Mine is a fast-moving cancer, Katy. I know what I've got, and it's a death sentence. I want to choose how I live the time I have left."

Craig looked helpless, like a lost child. He began to cry. Katy had never seen her father cry. It was devastating to her. She had all sorts of emotions flowing through her. Who had her father become?

"Why don't you go back to work, both of you?" Anne asked after a few moments. "Actually, Craig, I guess you'd better wait for the doctor, but please go back to work, Katy. It's best for us all. Your father can go back after he talks to the doctor."

"I took two weeks off, Anne. I was relieved of my position today and will be stationed in DC as I told you. It happened today and I'm actually relieved. I need to find out more about my new job at some point, but I'm on leave for now. There will be a press release today that might make tomorrow's paper in Aiken."

"My God, Dad! That's terrible. Can you tell me why again?"

"Well, it's just business, Katy. When something bad happens, whatever it is, it's always the contractor's fault. It's the deal we made with DOE. And anything that happens is also the fault of the GM. This one was bad enough to get me moved to DC. It's really just that simple."

"What about the inappropriate, sexual misconduct allegation? Is that part of this, and is it true?"

Craig had no idea what to say next. Even though he was struck by the devastation and disappointment in Katy's eyes, he struggled to find the words that would ease her pain.

"Well, first, no. They're not true, whatever they are. I don't know the specifics, but I've never come on to another woman since I married your mother, ever. I have no idea whether my boss buys the complaints or not, but I find it hard to believe he would, given my past. This sort of thing happens to guys like me from time to time. Someone's probably just trying to get a promotion or money from the company. The business is full of those types of people."

Katy stared at her dad, wanting desperately to believe him but somehow couldn't. If it had been a single allegation five years ago, she likely would have. But given his changed behavior over the past year, she could no longer dismiss it as impossible.

"Okay, Dad. I'm sorry that all this happened to you. I think I'll take Mom's advice and go back to work, especially since you're here with her now."

She gathered her things, bent over, and kissed her mother, then walked toward the door. Turning back to her parents before she left, she said, "I love you both."

As Katy drove back to work, her mind oscillated between the cancer her mother now faced and the shocking news from her father. The smell of the flowers Craig had brought to the room reminded her of the smell she loved so much when she visited them at home. The smell reminded her of her childhood where her mom and dad were always together and happy. It reminded her of the deep conversations between the three of them. Now she didn't know how to talk to either, especially her dad. He was distant and his words seemed forced and often inappropriate, not the fun-loving speak she had grown up with.

Anne and Craig spent the next few hours together, but little was said. Anne knew that something was wrong with Craig but didn't have the strength to think it through. She was dealing with her own mortality and all that surrounded it. She too sensed the way Craig's responses seemed forced.

The doctor eventually came in and gave Craig and Anne the specifics. He recommended starting chemotherapy the following week. With it, she could possibly add years to her life, if it went into remission; without it, she would likely pass in a year or two, at most. Craig listened with all his might and seemed to understand the situation but could not really put it in perspective well enough to help Anne make her decision. She told the doctor that she needed time to decide, to which her doctor replied there wasn't really a choice—chemo was her path forward. With soft but steely eyes, she thanked him and said she'd consider it. Craig simply went along with her wishes.

Craig and Anne went home and spent that evening and the next morning discussing their situations. Anne had prayed about her diagnosis, thought it over, and decided against chemo. Her odds were bleak, even with treatment. While it might prolong her life, the effects weren't worth it to her.

Katy came over the next morning before she went to her office to discuss her mother's path forward. As the three of them sat at the kitchen table, Anne explained her decision.

"I've decided to forego treatment," she began. "Please let me finish before you comment. You see, I actually believe in what we talk about all the time: faith. I have no idea why this happened to me; I just know that it did. And while I know you both will be praying with me for a healing, I'm ready to accept God's ultimate healing. Remember all the talks we've had over the years about eternity and how infinitely short our time here is, how time was created by God in Genesis when He said 'In the beginning' as a concept for us while we're here on Earth. Remember the discussions we've had on free will. Well, I believe all that and I'm ready to exercise that free will and exit this time constraint and move into eternity unless God intervenes otherwise."

Tears streamed down Katy's face. "My God, Mom, how can you say that? How can you not get treatment? You may live much longer, and we need you, Mom. We need you!"

Anne began to cry as well, but it was different. Her face was now not only a reflection of her only daughter's sorrow, but also of the iron resolve that had emerged from her faith. Her eyes showed compassion for her daughter, but not fear.

"Please know how much I love you, Katy, and how proud I am of you. But also please understand and accept my decision. I'm so certain of it. I feel a peace that I've never felt before. I'm not just being brave, Katy. I really mean it."

Craig was crying as well but said nothing. They all just sat at the table weeping.

I was never sure why she chose certain death over a long shot at life, but she had. The part that haunted me was whether Craig's conduct and situation at work had played in her decision. I knew she was aware of the changes Craig was going through and how hard her life would be with him. She had to face her friends and explain how her husband had fallen from a hero to an incompetent, sexual deviant. It may have all been too much for her, so she just gave up. I felt so guilty about it. I had failed in my attempts to keep Craig from his errors and mischief. Would God hold me accountable for that and for Anne's decision, or was she really so much stronger than we were and that Craig's errors were not part of her decision? Only God knew. Katy took Anne's decision like I did. She was shocked and blamed Craig. She had the same thoughts I had, which made my sorrow even greater.

Craig rented an apartment in DC not far from the corporate offices. He generally flew up on Monday mornings and flew home Friday evenings, though Dick allowed him to work from home when Craig needed to be with Anne. His job was ill-defined, and most days were inefficient. Dick couldn't use Craig to walk the halls of the Forestall to meet with DOE executives because of the events at Tritium, at least not for a year or so. Dick had asked Craig to help Fran with the recovery but to stay out of the line of sight of the customer. That had wounded Craig, but he stayed in contact with Fran, and she often bounced her plans off him.

Craig had also been assigned to various oversight groups. The company sent annual review teams to all its DOE contracts to look at how they were doing in safety, contamination control, compliance with the contract, and associated requirements. It was the kind of work Craig despised. He had always been on the other end of these reviews and hated them. He did little work while he was on the teams. The other team members thought he was just being an ass because of his fall from grace. While this may have been true to some extent, his dementia was the primary culprit. He just couldn't focus enough to make a contribution.

Some weeks later, Anne flew with Craig to DC, but the long days in the apartment alone were tough for her to take. She had lost all joy but remained strong in her faith. Her husband had become someone she didn't recognize, and her daughter had nearly totally withdrawn into her work. She was alone with God and her cancer.

CLARITY
Fall Leaves (2018)

Katy sat in her usual leather chair in the waiting room of Fall Leaves. It was five-thirty in the evening, and she was watching one of the caregivers halfheartedly attempt to feed her father. Betty too was watching the caregiver's every move. She even opened her mouth when the caregiver raised the spoon to Craig's mouth, an instinctive move much like a coach leaning his body to the right or left trying to will a field goal through the uprights.

Craig had been in Fall Leaves for nine years and was now one of the most progressed Emerald residents. Katy thought back to when she had moved him in and the painful period it was. Those had been dark days, and occasionally she still felt the pain of regret and shame over how she had handled the situation. Most days, however, she had a certain peace about the past, particularly from a self-respect standpoint. She knew that she had to be there regularly to ensure Craig was getting fed and cared for properly. She visited at least three times a week, putting his care on par with her job.

I could see how much Katy cared for him in her eyes, though she was now resigned to his fate. She realized there was nothing she could do except pray, and pray she did. I heard her prayers when Craig was in his trance-like state. She petitioned God for his healing, but I could tell her requests weren't totally sincere. However, when she prayed for Craig to find peace, the genuine depth of her pleading was obvious. She had gained perspective throughout this trial, for which I was grateful. As the days passed, I believed she would be relieved when we died. At first, the notion seemed wrong to me, but as time went on and I realized that my contact with Craig was all but gone, I saw the wisdom in it.

As she watched the drool drip from her father's lip while he took a bite of ground ham, Katy again felt that pang of remorse. There was no explaining her feelings, and they couldn't be suppressed, a roller coaster of emotions. At times, the cruelty of her dad's disease was unbearable. Other times, her dad would appear for a moment and say he loved her, filling her with warmth and joy. Other times still, the whole situation seemed comical. Katy couldn't always make sense of the ever-changing stream of emotions, so she just let them happen. She had put all of it in God's hands and knew it would be okay in the end. She just had to make it there.

Katy began to think about what it would be like when Craig passed. She knew she would mourn and be sorrowful, but she would also be relieved. For if she really believed what she said, then her dad would be with God, free from his failing body. She again contemplated Levi's questions about how a person like Craig could change personalities. Had the real Craig already gone on to be with God, or was he trapped inside, waiting to be rescued by death? She didn't have the answer, but she had a sense of peace that it was all going to be fine.

The caregiver had stopped feeding Craig and was just sitting at the table staring at her cell phone. Betty had finished eating and was staring at Craig. Katy got up and walked to the table. As the caregiver noticed her arrival, she picked up the spoon and again tried to get Craig to eat the pink meat.

"Is he not eating today?" Katy asked.

"Well, he ate almost half of his meal, but I think he's done."

Katy put her arm on Craig's shoulder and rubbed his neck. Craig turned his head slightly, seeming to acknowledge her touch. However, he said nothing, just stared past her as she caressed him.

NOWHERE TO HIDE
Tritium (2007)

In the time Craig had been in DC, his inability to do any type of real work had become quite apparent. He and his lack of contribution were the topic of his coworkers' conversations whenever he wasn't around. His daily routine consisted of coming to the office late, closing his door, and trying to respond to emails. His responses rarely made much sense.

Fran had been relieved of her duties at Tritium—a permanent replacement was now in Craig's old position—and had returned to DC. She'd heard what the others were saying, but refused to believe it—at first. However, soon after her return, she tried to apologize to Craig for taking over for him. It didn't go well. As soon as she started her apology, Craig went into a defensive diatribe about how it was simply operator error and that he was railroaded. Fran managed to leave the discussion intact, but didn't make another attempt to reconcile the way Craig felt with what she knew to be the truth. Craig's response had shocked her. He seemed more accepting while she was at Tritium and had actually contributed several helpful suggestions about the recovery. Still, she also recalled several emails from him that she could barely decipher.

Shortly after her run-in with Craig during her failed apology attempt, Fran was assigned the lead on an annual project review for one of their contracts at the Hanford site in Washington state. Dick assigned Craig to be part of her team. While others in the DC office warned Dick about how much Craig had changed, Dick said nothing. With very little contact with Craig, Dick simply let him "contribute" as he could until he found something at another site. Dick felt that Craig needed time to recover from the events at Tritium and hadn't really begun to look for another spot for him. He would just cover him on overhead until then.

Fran and Craig had always been close. She respected Craig. Replacing him at Tritium pained her, but she had no choice. However, Craig's conduct since then concerned her, and while she hadn't believed all of what the others were saying, she knew he was not the same person. Had he snapped from being replaced? Was he on a revenge tour? Other times, he seemed to be mired in a passive resistance mode. She wasn't looking forward to dealing with him during the review process.

Fran scheduled the review with their Hanford general manager, Rob Slacks, whom Fran knew well, sharing a reasonably good working relationship with him and his staff. The review was to last for one week, and she knew Rob would be cooperative, unless they found something of any significance. Rob was an ex-nuclear submarine commander, stood about five-foot-seven, and had a bit of a Napoleon complex. He walked about very erect and chewed unlit cigars when out in the facilities. His black hair was combed straight back, he wore pressed shirts, and his black patent leather shoes were always shined. He was a strong leader but could be defensive and dangerous when he felt cornered.

Fran negotiated the review criteria with Rob directly. She'd then forwarded the criteria to her team, including Craig. They were to fly out on Sunday evening and begin the review Monday morning. The team was staying at their usual hotel in Richland, Washington, by the river. Team members were flying in from other DOE sites the company ran. Dick felt that using other site personnel built teamwork for the company and allowed them to see other sites, and, of course, meant that he could keep his overhead staff as lean as possible.

Fran arrived on Sunday afternoon and checked into her room around five-thirty. The team was to meet at Geno's at Columbia Point. She reserved a table in the back, so the team could talk about the review and catch up on what was happening at the various sites. These were always fun meetings. Old friendships were rekindled over a great dinner and expensive wine, all paid for by overheads. What could be better?

After getting settled in her room, she called home and reviewed emails from her laptop. She then made her way to Geno's, which was a short walk from the hotel. She loved Richland and took a few minutes to appreciate the view of the Columbia River as she walked, noticing two aluminum boats making their way back to dock after a day of what she guessed was salmon fishing. Once at the restaurant, she checked in with the hostess and walked to the large table prepared for the group.

Slowly, all the others on the team arrived. Drinks flowed with lively conversations about problems, successes, and, most of all, the customer. By 7:15 p.m., the entire team had assembled, except Craig. Fran ordered wine and told the waitress they were still waiting on one more and they'd be ready to order dinner once he arrived.

Fifteen minutes later, there was still no sign of Craig. Fran discreetly pulled out her cell phone and called him. It went directly to voicemail, indicating he was either on another call or perhaps his phone was still in airplane mode. The group waited another fifteen minutes, then ordered dinner. They finished the last bottle of wine about two hours later. Craig was still a no-show.

As the group entered the hotel, Fran said her good-nights and told the group to get some rest because she wanted them hungry for issues the next day. She then walked to the front desk and asked if Craig had checked in. After checking the computer, the attendant reported he had just arrived. Fran thanked him and went to her room and called Craig again. This time he answered.

"You make it okay, Craig? Was your flight delayed?"

"No," said Craig. "Everything is fine."

"Well, you missed our dinner meeting. Last week, you responded to my email confirming that you'd meet us at Geno's tonight."

After a long and awkward pause, Craig replied that he hadn't received her email and that she must be mistaken. Fran felt aggravated by his incorrect response, knowing she had his reply still logged in her email batch, but she simply said, "Oh, I'm sorry, Craig. Just a simple miscommunication. You didn't miss much. I can catch you up in the morning. Would you like to ride over to the offices tomorrow with Ray and me? Ray's driving, and I can catch you up on the way."

"Sure," he replied quietly. "I'll meet you in the lobby tomorrow."

Craig sat on his bed after ending his call with Fran. His brain was firing out of control and he began to cry. He couldn't remember how he had gotten there, though there was a vague memory of having been lost trying to find the hotel. He remembered stopping for directions and having been told he had been driving in the wrong direction for nearly an hour. He somehow made it to where he was but couldn't remember how.

As he cried on his bed, I felt even more helpless and afraid than normal. Craig was a walking zombie, and I wasn't helping at all. I prayed and prayed, but Craig kept crying. What would tomorrow be like?

The morning was better. Craig made it downstairs and was ready for the ride to the company's site offices at Hanford. Fran thought he seemed a bit detached and noncommittal, but otherwise normal. Overall, the morning went well, and Craig actually engaged in a number of the discussions. However, after a break for lunch, Craig did not return. They began without him and were in the middle of reportable events that had been compiled by the Hanford team. As they talked, they were interrupted by a young executive assistant, who had Craig in tow.

"I think this one belongs to you," she said jokingly.

Everyone laughed as Craig sat down. His face was red and his brain was empty. He knew he was embarrassed but uncertain why. Linda found Craig sitting in the waiting area outside Rob's office reading emails on his phone. She'd asked if she could help him, eventually figured out who he was, and took him to the meeting.

Things can't go on like this, I thought. God, please send me some help. I'm clueless as to what to do for him. I need some help down here.

It was eleven the following Monday morning, the review team had completed its work in Hanford, and Fran and Craig were back in DC. Craig had first flown to Aiken from Richland after the review wrapped up, then went back to DC. He wanted to be with Anne over the weekend. Her condition was worsening.

Fran was in Dick's office going over the results of the review. The team hadn't really found much, except some issues around radiation protection. They saw a fairly significant spike in personnel contamination cases and suggested some corrective actions to improve donning and doffing protocols that seemed to be the cause. As she finished, Dick thanked her and asked if she had anything else. She paused.

"Well, yes, there is something else," she said.

"What is it?"

"It's Craig. As you know, you assigned him to our team."

"Yes, go on."

"I'm very worried about him. I'm not trying to rat him out. You know we're friends."

"Sure, I do, Fran. What is it?"

"Well, I'll just get to the point. I think Craig is sick, very sick. I've sensed it since I first took over Tritium, but to my regret and shame I took no action to try and help him. He didn't make it to our opening dinner meeting and said he never got an email that I know he got because he replied to it. He was essentially not there mentally for the entire review. Rob's assistant found him alone and in a daze outside Rob's office not knowing where he was."

Fran paused and tugged at her ear, frowning.

"I think he may have some very serious mental issues, Dick, maybe a form of dementia or perhaps he's having a breakdown of some sort. Either way, I'm worried. I'm worried for him and for us, to be frank. He's currently a walking liability. It's all over the office here, and the team members from the other sites noticed it too. It's terrible, Dick. We need to do something."

"Wow," said Dick. "That's concerning. I've noticed his mental withdrawal but thought perhaps he just needed to recover from his fall at Tritium. To be fully honest, I've tried hard to avoid him. It's always uncomfortable, and his rambling emails are so out of character. They used to be spot on, brief, and to the point. Now they're like a Dylan song."

They both smiled awkwardly.

"I'll give it some thought and do something, Fran, though I'm not sure what. Thanks for telling me; I know it wasn't easy."

***

Later that afternoon, Dick walked to Craig's office, knocked on the closed door, then opened it. Craig was in his chair looking out the window.

"Hey, Craig, got a minute?"

"Sure," he said as he turned toward Dick, who took a seat in a chair in front of Craig's desk.

"Is everything all right, Craig? You seem distracted. I understand you didn't seem to be yourself at the Hanford review. Just wanted to see if I can help."

"I'm fine. Why do you ask? Did Fran tell you something bad about the review? I think she's got it in for me. I noticed it when she took over Tritium."

"No. Fran didn't tell me anything bad about you. She is concerned, though, and so am I. You seem totally removed, Craig, like you're not engaged."

"I'm totally engaged. Why is everyone out to get me? You ran me out of Tritium and now you're trying to fire me, aren't you?"

Dick was taken aback but immediately realized just how bad things were. He knew not to confront Craig in his current state. "No one wants to fire you, but you may need some time to deal with this thing, whatever it is. I know Anne is very ill and maybe that's got you distracted. Would you like a week off to deal with it?"

"No, I'm fine. I just want to do my job."

"Okay, Craig," Dick said as he stood up. "Just relax. I'll let you get back to work. I just wanted to check in with you."

At that, Dick walked out and closed the door behind him. *Fran is right*, he thought. He returned to his office, closed his door, and wondered what he should do. Finally, he looked up Craig's contact information, found his home phone number, and dialed it.

"Hello?" said Katy, who had taken the day off to be with her mom.

"Hello. Is this Anne?"

"No, I'm Anne's daughter, Katy."

"Oh, hello, Katy. This is Dick, Craig's boss in DC. Can I talk to Anne?"

"I'm afraid not. She's resting right now."

"Um, all right. Well, Katy, I heard your mother is sick; is that right?"

"Yes, she is. She's in the final stage of cancer. Is there a problem with Dad, an accident or something?"

Dick paused. Should he tell her what he had intended to tell Anne? He knew that technically he should have called the company's employee concerns unit, but that was a painful process and would take weeks. "I'm so sorry to hear about Anne. Craig hasn't shared any of those details, and I'd have never called had I known. There was no accident, but there may be a problem. I wanted to discuss it with Anne."

"You can tell me, Dick. I'm pretty much running things here. Dad hasn't been able to deal with all this very well."

"That's actually why I'm calling. Your dad is not himself. He is almost totally withdrawn and very defensive. I'm going to have to do something about it, and whatever it is will require support from his family. I totally respect Craig. He's a good man and has been a tremendous asset to us. But I'm very worried about him."

"I think I know what you're talking about. He isn't the same person I've always known. I need to get involved because my mother can't."

"Okay, Katy. I really appreciate it."

"I can fly up to DC this week to discuss it, if you'd like. It's that important to me. I need to get him some help, and I need him back here to deal with Mom."

"That's nice of you. I'll give you my assistant's phone number, and you can make arrangements with her. She'll book and pay for your flight and any accommodations you need. I'll change my schedule to fit yours—just let her know what works best for you."

On Thursday afternoon, Katy was walking with Dick's executive assistant toward his office. She had been met at the outer door, and a path had been cleared to Dick's office so that Craig could in no way see her. They entered Dick's office, and Katy took a seat across from Dick at his conference table. Also at the table was a representative from the employee concerns section of the corporate human resources department.

At first, Katy was alarmed by the young man from employee concerns, but Dick assured her that everything discussed would be held in complete confidence and that the young man was there to help.

The meeting lasted nearly two hours. Katy covered her mom's cancer and how the Tritium event had changed their lives. She detailed how her dad was now no longer the dad she knew and asked for more information about the Tritium event and the employee grievances. Dick then reviewed Craig's removal from Tritium and gave a very brief and less-than-satisfying discussion of the concerns.

At the end of the meeting, the employee concerns rep recommended that Craig be tested for dementia. He felt it was their best first step, and, if true, Craig would be much better off than if he had to be removed from his job for cause. Katy agreed, saying she'd arrange the testing and keep them informed.

Katy lined up Craig's tests the following Monday. All her legal skills were needed to convince the doctor to take him on such short notice. She stayed at her parents' house the whole weekend, spending more time with Craig than she had in nearly a year. She convinced him to agree to the tests by stretching the truth. She told him that he might need help dealing with Anne and that it was simply a meeting to help them all get through it. Stretching the truth was a skill she would hone.

The tests had come back positive; the doctors diagnosed Craig with frontotemporal dementia. His prognosis was not good. While no one could be certain, the dementia looked to be progressing quickly and was exacerbated by the stress he had been under. Katy was saddened but also relieved that the father she loved had really been that man. He hadn't been an imposter after all. The change in him wasn't his fault. For that, she was so very grateful. She felt the guilt of having avoided him, thinking he was a hypocrite, and worse. But she also had his health to deal with along with her mom, who did not have long to live.

Katy had taken a two-week family leave from her firm, which worried her too. She knew the leave was due her, but actually taking it still concerned her; she needed to make partner next year, or she might be in trouble. Though on track, this sort of thing didn't help. Nevertheless, the firm assured her it was no issue and encouraged her to take as long as she needed. She was grateful for that.

I was grateful that things had worked out the way they had. God had heard my plea for assistance, and Katy was that help. I watched as she cared for Anne and Craig and saw that it changed her. She was thoughtful, putting her career and family on hold to care for her parents. Anne passed that year. She died in her sleep, and again, I was thankful. At the funeral, Craig's mind was normal again for nearly the entire time. He had thoughts of their first meeting, of Katy's birth, of coming home from work to Anne's beautiful face. He cried and cried. I cherished that time.

Katy arranged everything. She quietly contacted Dick and sent him the paperwork associated with Craig's diagnosis. Dick had been helpful in getting Craig's retirement through their system and had optimized all his compensation. Katy convinced Craig that he should retire, though he really didn't understand what happened. Craig then moved back to Aiken and was with Anne for the last months of her life.

Katy was in charge, much to my relief.

After Anne passed, Craig lived in Aiken for nearly two years with a visiting nurse. As his dementia progressed, Katy eventually convinced Craig to move into Fall Leaves, telling him he needed to move into an apartment now that Mom was gone and he was alone. He initially resisted but came around as Katy spun her helpful stretches of the truth. She would have liked to have him move in with her and her family, but there was no way. Craig needed more care than she could give. She knew she made the only decision possible, and yet it haunted her.

NO NEED TO HIDE
Fall Leaves (2018)

It's been a good life, I thought, as Craig lay sleeping next to Betty. All the tiny and monumental moments of life with Craig were in perspective, and I was thankful for them. Our parents had been the kind others envied. They raised us up in the ways of God and cared for us with love, wisdom, and compassion. Though our childhood was followed by the rebellion and poor choices of early adulthood, God had always seen us through. We shared our days with a beautiful, supportive wife, good friends, and a devoted, treasured daughter. We had worked diligently for success in our career and home. For this full life, I was most grateful.

The malfunctioning of Craig's mind was no longer life-shattering to me. Though I was rendered useless, things worked out with the passage of time. As I lost control, Katy found within herself the skill and compassion needed to be our caregiver, which then brought a rewarding sense of fulfillment. Levi found God through the strange, but beneficial relationship between Betty and Craig, and he found friendship with Thomas and Katy, strengthening their faith as iron sharpens iron.

I was compelled to thank God for it all, all the experiences, all the moments, all the time, all the love. The difficult and dark times had faded; I could barely remember them. Peace engulfed me.

Suddenly, I felt a feeling I had never experienced before, as if I had awoken abruptly from a vivid dream and could barely distinguish between the dream and reality. I somehow realized that Craig had stopped breathing and that his brain function was no longer active. Betty was shaking his shoulder and calling his name, but he did not respond. She shook him harder and harder and then began to scream.

In what seemed like only a few seconds, Thomas arrived.

"What is it, Miss Betty?" he asked after barging though the door. Betty said nothing but was now weeping loudly. Thomas went to the bed and tried to rouse Craig. Again, no response.

"My God! My God!" Thomas exclaimed as he turned and ran out the door toward the nurses' station. "Call 911. Mr. Craig is not responding; I think he may have passed. He's already pale."

The nurse, Thomas, and several other caregivers were waiting as the paramedics arrived only fifteen minutes later. They took his vitals, but it was clear that Craig had gone on hours before. Betty was sitting on the love seat, weeping loudly.

"He's gone," one of the paramedics said. "We'll take him to the hospital, so please notify his next of kin."

"I've already done that," Thomas said. "She will be here soon."

Katy was on her way, weeping as she drove. "Why did he die, Lord?" she cried out. "Why?" But then she felt her Spirit being corrected. She paused and remembered that she had prayed for God to take her dad whenever He deemed fit because his life had become terrible. She dried her eyes and began to pray out loud. "I'm so sorry, God. I'm so sorry. I just said what I said without thinking. Thank you for my dad and all that he has meant to me. I love him so and am so very glad he's with you now." She continued to weep as she drove, but it was not the same. A mix of emotions—not unlike what she'd seen in her mother's eyes the day they wept over her decision to forgo treatment—that included sorrow, relief, and perhaps even a touch of joy drove her tears.

I was aware of all that was happening. I wasn't sure how because normally I only saw what Craig saw, but he was gone. Where was I and who was I? I watched as the paramedics dragged Craig's limp body onto the gurney and then rolled him to the elevator. I watched as Betty wept. I watched as Thomas prayed for Katy as he saw her coming from the elevator toward the paramedics wheeling her father's dead body. I watched as she fell to her knees weeping after she saw her father's body. I watched as Thomas knelt beside her and hugged her and wept with her.

How was I so aware of all this? Where was I? What should I do?

Suddenly, I was no longer concerned about the events before me. I felt an incredible, indescribable peace, a peace I'd never known. All was completely perfect, and I had the sense that nothing could ever be wrong again. I felt no worries, no cares. Even the traumatic events I had just witnessed seemed insignificant. I was floating in a sea of total peace. Feelings of euphoria rolled like waves over me. But if this feeling wasn't enough, I also had an indescribable and overwhelming feeling of anticipation. I was certain much more was to come, and it would be better than anything I could imagine. I knew it was coming and couldn't wait, but somehow I also knew that the peace I now felt would be enough to sustain me until what I was anticipating came to be.

Whatever it was would have to wait, and I was more than happy to wait as long as I felt this peace. I seemed to be moving but wasn't sure. I no longer felt tied in any way to the events before me. I was free of them and moving to another place. I was unaware of where I was going or even where I was. But as I rested, I began to reflect on what had happened. I wasn't sad, but I simply wondered about Katy, about Thomas, and about Craig. Where was Craig now?

As I contemplated my questions, a strong rush of peace swept over me, and I heard a voice within my being say to me, "Craig was a temporary vessel, a test that I prepared for you. Well done. Now rest in my peace until I'm ready for you."